FEN COUNTRY

FEN COUNTRY

Twenty-six stories

by

EDMUND CRISPIN

WALKER AND COMPANY
NEW YORK

First published in the United States of America
in 1980 by the Walker Publishing Company, Inc.

ISBN: 0-8027-5424-4

Library of Congress Catalog Card Number: 80-51723

Printed in the United States of America

10 9 8 7 6 5 4 3 2 1

ACKNOWLEDGEMENTS

The following stories were first published in the *Evening Standard*:
After Evensong (1953), Blood Sport (1954), A Case in Camera
(1955), A Country to Sell (1955), Death and Aunt Fancy (1953),
Dog in the Night-Time (1954), Gladstone's Candlestick (1955),
The House by the River (1953), The Hunchback Cat (1954), The
Lion's Tooth (1955), Man Overboard (1954), The Man Who Lost
His Head (1955), Merry-Go-Round (1953), Occupational Risk
(1955), Shot in the Dark (1952), The Two Sisters (1955), The
Undraped Torso (1954), Who Killed Baker? (1950), Windhover
Cottage (1954), Wolf! (1953), The Pencil (1953). The following
appeared in *Ellery Queen's Mystery Magazine:* Death Behind Bars
© Edmund Crispin 1960, Outrage in Stepney © Edmund Crispin
1955. The following stories appeared in *Winter's Crimes*: The
Mischief Done © Edmund Crispin 1972, We Know You're Busy
Writing . . . © Edmund Crispin 1969. The following story has
not previously been published: Cash On Delivery © Barbara
Montgomery 1979.

CONTENTS

1 Who Killed Baker? by Edmund Crispin and Geoffrey Bush   9

2 Death and Aunt Fancy   16

3 The Hunchback Cat   21

4 The Lion's Tooth   26

5 Gladstone's Candlestick   31

6 The Man Who Lost His Head   36

7 The Two Sisters   42

8 Outrage in Stepney   47

9 A Country to Sell   52

10 A Case in Camera   57

11 Blood Sport   62

12 The Pencil   66

13 Windhover Cottage   70

14 The House by the River   75

15 After Evensong   79

16 Death Behind Bars   83

17 We Know You're Busy Writing, But We Thought You Wouldn't Mind If We Just Dropped In For A Minute   92

18 Cash on Delivery   108

19 Shot in the Dark   113

20 The Mischief Done   118

21 Merry-Go-Round   133

22 Occupational Risk   137

23 Dog in the Night-Time   142

24 Man Overboard   147

25 The Undraped Torso   152

26 Wolf!   157

FEN COUNTRY

WHO KILLED BAKER?

by Edmund Crispin and Geoffrey Bush

WAKEFIELD WAS ATTENDING a series of philosophy lectures at London University, and for the past ten minutes his fellow-guests at Haldane's had been mutely enduring a *précis* of the lecturer's main contentions.

"What it amounts to, then," said Wakefield, towards what they hoped was the close of what they hoped was his peroration, "is that philosophy deals not so much with the answers to questions about Man and the Universe as with the problem of *what questions may properly be asked.* Improper questions"—here a little man named Fielding, whom no one knew very well, choked suddenly over his port and had to be led out—"improper questions can only confuse the issue. And it's this aspect of philosophy which in my opinion defines its superiority to other studies, such as—such as"—Wakefield's eye lighted on Gervase Fen, who was stolidly cracking walnuts opposite—"such as, well, criminology, for instance."

Fen roused himself.

"Improper questions," he said reflectively. "I remember a case which illustrates very clearly how——"

"Defines," Wakefield repeated at a higher pitch, "its superiority to——"

But at this point, Haldane, perceiving that much more of Wakefield on epistemology would certainly bring the party to a premature end, contrived adroitly to upset his port into Wakefield's lap, and in the mêlée which ensued it proved possible to detach the conversational initiative from Wakefield and confer it on Fen.

"Who killed Baker?" With this rather abrupt query Fen established a foothold while Wakefield was still scrubbing ineffectually at his damp trousers with a handkerchief. "The situation which resulted in Baker's death wasn't in itself specially

complicated or obscure, and in consequence the case was solved readily enough."

"Yes, it would be, of course," said Wakefield sourly, "if you were solving it."

"Oh, but I wasn't." Fen shook his head decisively, and Wakefield, shifting about uncomfortably in the effort to remove wet barathea from contact with his skin, glowered at him. "The case was solved by a very able Detective Inspector of the County CID, by name Casby, and it was from him that I heard of it, quite recently, while we were investigating the death of that Swiss schoolmaster at Cotten Abbas. As nearly as I can, I'll tell it to you the way he told me. And I ought to warn you in advance that it's a case in which the mode of telling is important—as important, probably, as the thing told. . . .

"At the time of his death Baker was about forty-five, a self-important little man with very black, heavily-brilliantined hair, an incipient paunch, dandified clothes, and a twisted bruiser's nose which was the consequence not of pugnacity but of a fall from a bicycle in youth. He was not, one gathers, at all a pleasing personality, and he had crowned his dislikeable qualities by marrying, and subsequently bullying, a wife very much younger and more attractive than himself. For a reason which the sequel will make obvious, there's not much evidence as to the form this bullying took, but it was real enough—no question about that—and three years of it drove the wretched woman, more for consolation than for passion, into the arms of the chauffeur, a gloomy, sallow young man named Arnold Snow. Since Snow had never read D. H. Lawrence, his chief emotion in the face of Mary Baker's advances was simple surprise, and to do him justice, he seems never to have made the smallest attempt to capitalize his position in any of the obvious ways. But, of course, the neighbours talked; there are precedents enough for such a relationship's ending in disaster."

Haldane nodded. "Rattenbury," he suggested, "and Stoner."

"That sort of thing, yes. It wasn't a very sensible course for Mary Baker to adopt, the more so as for religious reasons she had a real horror of divorce. But she was one of those warm, good-natured, muddle-headed women—not, in temperament, unlike Mrs Rattenbury—to whom a man's affection is overwhelmingly necessary, as much for emotional as for physical reasons; and three years of Baker had starved that side of her so effectively that when she did break out, she broke out with a vengeance. I've seen a photograph of her, and can tell you that she was rather a big woman (though not fat), as dark as her husband or her lover, with a large mouth and eyes, and a Rubensish figure. Why she married Baker in the first place I really can't make out. He was well-to-do—or, anyway, seemed so—but Mary was the sort of woman to whom money quite genuinely means nothing; and oddly enough, Snow seems to have been as indifferent to it as she.

"Baker was a manufacturer. His factory just outside Twelford made expensive model toys—ships, aeroplanes, cars, and so forth. The demand for such things is strictly limited—people who know the value of money very properly hesitate before spending fifteen guineas on a toy which their issue are liable to sit on, or drop into a pond, an hour later—and when Philip Eckerson built a factory in Ruislip for producing the same sort of thing, only more cheaply, Baker's profits dropped with some abruptness to rather less than half what they'd been before. So for five years there was a price-war—a price-war beneficial to the country's nurseries, but ruinous to Baker and Eckerson alike. When eventually they met, to arrange a merger, both of them were close to bankruptcy.

"It was on 10 March of this year they met—not on neutral territory, but in Baker's house at Twelford, where Eckerson was to stay the night. Eckerson was an albino, which is uncommon, but apart from that the only remarkable thing about him was obstinacy, and since he confined this trait to business, the impression he made on Mary Baker during his visit to her house was in every respect colourless. She was aware, in a vague, general way, that he was her husband's business rival, but she bore him not the least malice on that account; and as to Snow, the mysteries of finance were beyond him, and from first to last he never understood how close to the rocks his employer's affairs had drifted. In any case, neither he nor Mary Baker had much attention to spare for Eckerson, because an hour or two before Ecker-·son arrived Baker summoned the pair of them to his study, informed them that he knew of their liaison, and stated that he would take steps immediately to obtain a divorce.

"It's doubtful, I think, if he really intended to do anything of the kind. He didn't sack Snow, he didn't order his wife out of the house, and apparently he had no intention of leaving the house himself—all of which would amount, in law, to condoning his wife's adultery and nullifying the suit. No, he was playing cat-and-mouse, that was all; he knew his wife's horror of divorce, and wished quite simply to make her miserable for as long as the pretence of proceedings could be kept up; but neither Mary nor Snow had the wit to see that he was duping them for his own pleasure, and they assumed in consequence that he meant every word he said. Mary became hysterical—in which condition she confided her obsession about divorce to Snow. And Snow, a remarkably naïve and impressionable young man, took it all *au grand sérieux*. He had not, up to now, displayed any notable animus against Baker, but Mary's terror and wretchedness fanned hidden fires, and from then on he was implacable. They were a rather pitiful pair, these two young people cornered by an essentially rather trivial issue, but their very ignorance made them dangerous, and if Baker had had more sense he'd never have played such an imbecile trick on them. Psychologically, he was certainly in a morbid condition, for apparently he was prepared to let the relationship go on, provided he could indulge his sadistic instincts in this weird and preposterous fashion. What the end of it all would have been, if death hadn't intervened, one doesn't, of course, know.

"Well, in due course Eckerson arrived, and Mary entertained him as well as her emotional condition would allow, and he sat up with Baker till the small hours, talking business. The two men antagonized one another from the start; and the more they talked, the more remote did the prospect of a merger become, until in the latter stages all hope of it vanished, and they went to their beds on the very worst of terms, with nothing better to look forward to than an extension of their present cut-throat competition, and eventual ruin. You'd imagine that self-interest would be strong enough, in a case like that, to compel them to some sort of agreement, but it wasn't—and of course the truth of the matter is that each was hoping that, if competition continued, the other would crack first, leaving a clear field. So they parted on the landing with mutual, and barely concealed, ill-will; and the house slept.

"The body was discovered shortly after nine next morning,

and the discoverer was Mrs Blaine, the cook. Unlike Snow, who lived in, Mrs Blaine had a bed-sitting-room in the town; and it was as she was making her way round to the back door of Baker's house, to embark on the day's duties, that she glanced in at the drawing-room window and saw the gruesome object which lay in shadow on the hearth-rug. Incidentally, you mustn't waste any of your energy suspecting Mrs Blaine of the murder; I can assure you she had nothing to do with it, and I can assure you, too, that her evidence, for what little it was worth, was the truth, the whole truth, and nothing but the truth. . . .

"Mrs Blaine looked in at the window, and her first thought, to use her own words, 'was that 'e'd fainted'. But the streaks of blood on the corpse's hair disabused her of this notion without much delay, and she hurried indoors to rouse the household. Well, in due course Inspector Casby arrived, and in due course assembled such evidence as there was. The body lay prone on a rug soaked with dark venous blood, and the savage cut which had severed the internal jugular vein had obviously come from behind, and been wholly unexpected. Nearby, and innocent of fingerprints, lay the sharp kitchen knife which had done the job. Apart from these things, there was no clue.

"No clue, that is, of a positive sort. But there *had* been an amateurish attempt to make the death look like a consequence of burglary—or rather, to be more accurate, of housebreaking. The pane of a window had been broken, with the assistance of flypaper to prevent the fragments from scattering, and a number of valuables were missing. But the breakfast period is not a time usually favoured by thieves, there were no footprints or marks of any kind on the damp lawn and flower bed beneath the broken window (which was not, by the way, the window through which Mrs Blaine had looked, but another, at right angles to it, on a different side of the house), and finally—and in Inspector Casby's opinion, most conclusive of all—one of the objects missing was a tiny but very valuable bird-study by the Chinese emperor Hui Tsung, which Baker, no connoisseur or collector of such things, had inherited from a great-uncle. The ordinary thief, Casby argued, would scarcely give a Chinese miniature a second glance, let alone remove it. No, the burglary was bogus; and unless you postulated an implausibly sophisticated double-bluff, then the murder had been done by one of the three people sleeping in the house. As to motive—well, you know all about that already; and one way and another it didn't take Inspector Casby more than 24 hours to make his arrest."

Somewhat grudgingly, Fen relinquished the walnuts and applied himself to stuffed dates instead. His mouth full, he looked at the company expectantly; and with equal expectancy the company looked back at him. It was Wakefield who broke the silence.

"But that can't be *all*," he protested.

"Certainly it's all," said Fen. "I've told you the story as Inspector Casby told it to me, and I now repeat the question he asked me at the end of it—and which I was able to answer, by the way: *Who killed Baker?*"

Wakefield stared mistrustfully. "You've left something out."

"Nothing, I assure you, If anything, I've been rather more generous with clues than Inspector Casby was. But if you still have no idea who killed Baker, I'll give you another hint: he died at 9 am. Does that help?"

They thought about this. Apparently it didn't help in the least.

"All right," Wakefield said sulkily at last. "We give up. Who killed Baker?"

And Fen replied blandly, "The public executioner killed him—after he had been tried and convicted for the murder of Eckerson."

For a moment Wakefield sat like one stupefied; then he emitted a howl of rage. "Unfair!" he shouted, banging on the table. "Trickery!"

"Not at all." Fen was unperturbed. "It's a trick story, admittedly, but you were given ample warning of that. It arose out of a discussion about the propriety of asking certain questions; and there was only one question—*Who killed Baker?*—which I asked. What's more, I emphasized at the outset that the mode of telling was as important as the thing told.

"But quite apart from all that, you had your clue. Mrs Blaine, looking in through a window at a figure lying in shadow, concluded that violence had been done for the reason that she saw blood on the hair. Now that blood, as I mentioned, was dark venous blood; and I mentioned also that Baker had black, heavily-brilliantined hair. Is it conceivable that dark blood would be *visible* on such hair—visible, that is, when the body was in shadow and the observer outside the window of the room in which it lay? Of course not. Therefore, the body was not Baker's. But it couldn't have been Mary Baker's, or Snow's, since they too were black-haired—and that leaves only Eckerson. Eckerson was an albino, which means that his hair was white; and splotches of blood would show up on white hair all right—even though it was in shadow, and Mrs Blaine some distance away. Who, then, would want to kill Eckerson? Baker, obviously, and Baker alone—I emphasized that both Snow and Mary were quite indifferent to the visitor. And who, after the arrest, would be likely to kill (notice, please, that I never at any time said 'murder') Baker? There's only one possible answer to that. . . ."

"And what happened to the wife?" Haldane asked. "Did she marry Snow?"

"No. He melted," said Fen complacently, "away. She married someone else, though, and according to Inspector Casby is very happy now. Baker's and Eckerson's businesses both collapsed under heavy debts, and no longer exist."

There was a pause; then: "The nature of existence," said Wakefield suddenly, "has troubled philosophers in all ages. What are the sensory and mental processes which cause us to assert that this table, for instance, is *real*? The answer given by the subjective idealists——"

"Will have to wait," said Haldane firmly, "till we meet again." He pushed back his chair. "Let's go and see what the women are up to, shall we?"

DEATH AND AUNT FANCY

THE WOMAN WHO opened the door of the cottage to George Gotobed's knock was big-boned, active-looking, tubular-shaped: somewhere in the late fifties or early sixties, with a booming voice.

"Mr Gotobed?" she greeted him. "My name is Preedy, and I am your aunt's companion. Do step inside. We're still in a bit of a muddle, I'm afraid. You'll have to remember that it's only three days since we moved in, and make allowances for us.

"But so cosy, don't you think, and you must speak up a bit" —this in response to some muttered civility of George's— "because we're both hard of hearing, though your aunt has one of these deaf-aid things, no use for them myself—this way, and you'd better leave your hat on that chair."

George Gotobed's Aunt Fancy, whom he was meeting for the first time, proved to be of a different order of beings from her companion. She was a little plump robin of a woman, wearing a brooch-spangled frock of unsuitable blue and sitting huddled defensively on a sofa.

Beside her a small radio set discoursed light music in a low murmur. If she were deaf, George asked himself, how on earth could she hear the thing?—and only then noticed the deaf-aid plugged into her ear.

And now she, too, was murmuring at him, uttering the conventional greetings, asking the expected questions. Infected by her diplomatic undertones, George answered in kind—until Miss Preedy impatiently requested them both to speak up: after which they shouted.

But it was not until Miss Preedy went to the kitchen to fetch in the tea that the curious incident occurred. As the door closed behind the companion, the expression on Aunt Fancy's mild features altered abruptly, giving place to one of alarm.

"George—Mr Gotobed," she whispered, "you mustn't leave me. I don't know why she's doing this." Her eyes shifted. "I'm frightened," she said. "Don't go away, will you? Stay the night. Please, please don't go a——"

And at that she broke off, for the door had opened and Miss Preedy was back. For heaven's sake, thought George, is this meant to be a joke? Or is the old girl a bit loopy?

As he sat there uncomfortably sipping his tea, with the muted tones of Quilter and Eric Coates still filling the air, he found that for the life of him he was unable to take his aunt's words seriously. Of course, there had been old ladies whose companions had murdered them for their money. But apparently Aunt Fancy wasn't well off these days, and—— No, no; ridiculous.

They ate and drank and talked politely, and presently George rose to take his leave. The invitation to stay, he noted, was not renewed; and he was steadfast in avoiding his aunt's eye. Persecution mania, he reflected, as he walked back to the village: poor old thing.

But he always wondered, looking back on it afterwards, how far he had really, in his inmost heart, believed that.

Since it was impossible for him to get back to Oxford that night, he had booked a room at the village inn, intending to make the journey in the morning. But in actual fact it was 48 hours or more before he reappeared at his college.

"So there I was, sir, stuck with it," he told his tutor. "Aunt Fancy smothered with her own pillow during the night, the cottage burgled, policemen and lawyers to see, the body to identify—what with one thing and another, I was lucky to get away as soon as I did."

"My dear George," said the tutor, whose name was Gervase Fen, "there's no need to apologize. Without wishing to be unkind, I may say that all this is vastly more entertaining than your opinions on *The Merchant of Venice*. Of course, I'm very sorry about your aunt——"

"That's all right, sir," George interrupted him. "I can't say I'm all that cut up about it—except, of course, for the fact that I deliberately ignored her appeal for help; that's not so funny. No, the point about it is that I'd never seen the old lady before, and she wasn't really my aunt even—she was my step-father's sister —so naturally I don't feel——"

"Just so. Am I right in thinking that she was your only remaining relative?"

"Yes, sir."

"Natural enough, then, that she should remember you in her will."

"Well, sir, not quite so natural as all that. You see, when my step-father was alive she quarrelled with him violently. And she's never once written to me till just the other day, when she asked me to come and see her; so I certainly wasn't expecting to inherit anything from her."

"Yes. Interesting. Let me get this straight, now. As I understand it, your aunt went out to Kenya some 40 years ago and remained there solidly up till last month, when she embarked for England. Incidentally, why the move? Any particular reason?"

"I gather she was running out of cash, sir. And if she'd got to pocket her pride and live on a more modest scale she preferred it to be in England, among strangers."

"I see. But in that case your inheritance——"

"Life insurance, sir: there's a big sum to come in life insurance. The companion—Miss Preedy—gets half, and I get the other half." George hesitated; then burst out: "Look here, sir, who do you think did the murder? Was it a burglar? Or was it Miss Preedy?"

"Neither," said Fen promptly. "Have you a photograph of your aunt?"

George shook his head, bewildered. "I haven't, I'm afraid. But——"

"Then we must rely," Fen interposed, "on Dawkins—an ex-pupil of mine. For some years now Dawkins has been living and working in Nairobi. Also, he is an indefatigable diner-out. You can take it from me that there is no one more likely to be able to give me the facts about your aunt and Miss Preedy than Dawkins."

Fen rose. "The cablegram service is quick," he observed, "so I think that if you were to come back in, say, a couple of hours——"

And two hours later the reply had, in fact, arrived. "FANCY LOOMIS FAIRLY DEAF," George read with astonishment, "PREEDY NOT DEAF AT ALL GREETINGS DAWKINS. But what does it mean, sir?" George demanded helplessly.

Fen grunted. "We shall have to confirm it by wiring photographs to Kenya," he said, "and I've already rung up the police, and they've agreed to that. But from what you've told me, I've no doubt about the result."

"I just don't understand, sir."

"Oh, come, George. Surely even you realize by now that the person you thought was Miss Preedy is in fact your aunt: and the person you thought was your aunt was in fact Miss Preedy?

"Nor," Fen went on, "is there much difficulty about the motive. Here is your aunt, running out of money, with the life insurance her only possible resource. So what does she do? Answer: she comes with Miss Preedy to England, where they aren't known, swaps rôles, and commits murder with a view to inheriting half the life insurance."

Fen reached for a cigarette. "You were brought into it as legatee and as visitor to the cottage, in order to diffuse a suspicion which must otherwise have been fairly concentrated. And in case for any reason that failed, the burglary was faked to make a supplementary red herring.

"How your aunt persuaded Miss Preedy to the substitution we shall probably never know. But to judge from your description, Miss Preedy was a very biddable person, very much under your aunt's thumb. '*I don't know why she's doing this.*' Poor creature, she had her suspicions, even so."

"But how did you know, sir?"

"The radio, George," said Fen. "The radio, of course. It was playing quietly, you remember. Your 'aunt' had a deaf-aid on, too.

"Now, you were talking to her—to start with, anyway—in a low voice. If she was in fact deaf, then the deaf-aid must have been amplifying your voice considerably.

"But in that case, it was also amplifying the radio. *If* the woman you were speaking to was genuinely deaf—genuinely using the deaf-aid—then the radio must all the time have sounded quite loud to her, even though it sounded quiet to you.

"Can you conceive anyone so circumstanced speaking to you in a low voice, whispering to you? Do you naturally speak to people in a low voice, when you have the radio on loud?

"So the answer was obvious: the woman you spoke to wasn't deaf at all. And once I realized that a trick had been played, it didn't take much inquiry to find out why."

Fen sighed. "Yes, I'm sorry, George; your Aunt Fancy is going to hang. And it's *The Merchant*, after all, which has the last word."

"Shakespeare, sir?"

"Shakespeare. Let us," said Fen, "all ring Fancy's knell."

THE HUNCHBACK CAT

"WE'RE *all* SUPERSTITIOUS," said Fen. And from the assembled party, relaxing by the fire, rose loud cries of dissent. "But we are, you know," Fen persisted, "whether we realize it or not. Let me give you a test."

"All right," they said. "Do."

"Let me tell you about the Copping case."

"A crime," they gloated. "Good."

"And if any of you," said Fen, "can solve it unassisted, he (or she, of course) shall be held to be without stain.

"The Copping family was an old one, and like most old families it had its traditions, the most important of these being, unfortunately, parricide.

"This didn't always take the form of actual *murder*. Sometimes it was accident, and sometimes it was neglect, and sometimes Copping parents were driven by the insufferable behaviour of their offspring to open a vein in the bath. None the less, there it was. As the toll mounted with the years, the Coppings inevitably became more and more prone to brood.

"By 1948, however, there were only two Coppings in the direct line left alive—Clifford Copping, a widower, and his daughter Isobel. Isobel, moreover, was married, and consequently no longer lived in the family mansion near Wantage. In August of 1948, however, she and her husband went to Wantage for a short visit. And that was when the thing happened.

"As for me, I was making a dètour through Wantage, on my way back from Bath to Oxford, so as to be able to have dinner at the White Hart. And it was in the bar of the White Hart, at shortly after six in the evening, that I got into conversation with Isobel's husband, Peter Doyle. He was drinking a fair amount. And by a quarter to eight he had reached the stage of insisting that I return with him to the Copping house for a meal.

"I didn't at all want to do that, but as he already knew that I'd been proposing to dine at the pub, alone, it was difficult to refuse.

So in the end I gave in, and we set out to walk to the house by way of the fields.

"It was a beautiful evening: I enjoyed the walk thoroughly. There was a cat, a handsome little high-stepping tortoiseshell cat, which adopted us, following us the whole way. 'She seems to want to come in,' I said when we arrived at the front door. And, 'That's all right,' said Doyle vaguely. 'Isobel and my father-in-law are both fond of cats.' So she did come in, and she and I were introduced to Isobel together.

"I quite liked Isobel. But it was clear from the first that relations between her and her husband were very strained. We all talked commonplaces for a while, and then Doyle suggested that as there was still a little time to use up before dinner, he should take me to meet his father-in-law, who would probably not be joining us for the meal.

" 'He hasn't been too well recently,' Doyle explained. 'You know, broody, a bit . . . But he'd never forgive me if I let you go away without his meeting you.'

"Well, of course I mumbled the usual things about not wanting to be a nuisance and so forth. And I can tell you, I should have been a good deal more emphatic about them if I'd known then what the inquest subsequently brought out: that for a long time now Clifford Copping had been seriously neurotic, with suicidal tendencies . . . However, I didn't know, so I allowed myself to be over-ruled. Her father was in the top room of the tower, Isobel said. So to the tower, still accompanied by our faithful cat, Doyle and I duly went.

"It stood apart from the rest of the house, 50 feet high or more, with smooth sheer walls and narrow slits for windows; date about 1450, I should think. I expected it to be fairly ruinous inside, but surprisingly, it wasn't. On the top landing Doyle paused in front of a certain door. I was a little way behind him, still negotiating the last flight of stairs.

" 'If you don't mind waiting a moment, 'I'll just go in and warn him that you're here,' he said—a proposal which didn't seem to me to march very well with his assurance, earlier on, that his father-in-law would never forgive him if I left without being introduced. However, of course, I agreed—whereupon he produced from his pocket a key which I'd seen Isobel give him, and proceeded to unlock (yes, definitely it *was* locked) and to half-open the door. He looked back at me then, saying in a low voice:

" 'I expect you'll think it's odd, but my father-in-law does like to be locked in here from time to time, so long as it's Isobel who keeps the key: he trusts Isobel completely. Being shut in, and having these tremendously thick walls all around him—it gives him a feeling of security. Of course, locking him*self* in is what he'd really like best, but the doctor won't allow that. That's why all the bolts have been taken away.'

" 'Ah,' I said. And something of what I felt must have showed in my face, because Doyle added:

" 'He's all right, you know . . . But naturally, if you—I mean, would you rather we didn't?'

" '*Yes, I'd very much rather,*' would have been the truthful answer to that. But Doyle's question was plainly of a piece with the Latin *Num?*: it expected a negative—and got one. So then we stopped talking, and while I waited nervously on the stair, Doyle entered the room. And found the body.

"Actually, to be just and exact about it, it was the cat which saw the body first. While we'd been talking, the cat had been looking into the room, and not at all liking what was in there. You know how they arch their backs, and the hair stands up all over the spine . . . ? Well, after about a minute and a half, or perhaps as much as two minutes, Doyle came out again, very slow and white and shaken, and sat down on the top stair with his head in his hands. I could have asked him questions, but I didn't. I went past him into the room and saw for myself.

"There was a kitchen knife and a severed throat and an almost inconceivable mess of blood. When I'd satisfied myself that no one was hidden there (and also that not even a child could possibly have escaped through the tiny windows) I felt Copping's skin and looked at the blood and concluded (correctly, as it turned out) that the wretched man had been dead at least an hour (it was then 8.24 exactly). Then I locked the room again and gave the key back to Doyle, and together we returned to the house, where he telephoned the police and a doctor while I went off on my own and—well, you can guess what I did, can't you?

"The rest is easily told. Copping had last been seen alive at 6.15, by Isobel when she locked him into the tower room; also he'd been seen not more than five minutes before that by two of the servants—so if there was any question of murder, at least it was certain that Doyle hadn't done it . . .

"And fortunately there *was* some question of murder—very much so. True, there were no prints except Copping's own on the knife. But low down on one of the panels of the room you could see traces of the blood, as if a splashed skirt-hem, say. had brushed against it . . . That wasn't done by Doyle or myself; there was no blood on either of us, anywhere. And it wasn't done by Copping in his death-agony—for the simple reason that between the body and the panel a considerable area of floor was innocent of blood-spots.

"All of which meant Isobel.

"Isobel who had had the key of that virtually impregnable room. Isobel who would inherit the whole of her father's estate. Isobel in whose wardrobe, hastily hidden away, the police found a stained mackintosh . . .

"That's really the lot. I told the CID my story, just as I've told it to you. And do you know, at the end of it, they were *still* proposing to arrest Isobel . . . Sheer superstition." Fen got to his feet. "Well, it's been a delightful evening, but I think I'd better be getting along now . . ."

The resultant howl nearly deafened him. He shook his head at them mock-mournfully. "No true rationalists? Really none? But unless you happen to be superstitious, it's simple. Doyle's wife was preparing to divorce him, you see, thereby depriving him of his chance of a share in all that lovely inheritance. He hated her bitterly for that, and in his father-in-law's death he saw a chance of revenge. It was he, of course, who planted the stained mackintosh, in the interim before the arrival of the police: I know that much because by then I'd realized what he was up to, and quite simply followed and watched him, without his being aware of it . . ."

"But Gervase, you haven't explained anything," wailed a fair-haired girl plaintively. "What *we* want to know is what made you suspicious of him in the first place."

Fen laughed. "Oh come now. You're none of you superstitious, you've assured me of that. And not being superstitious, you ought to be aware that it's only in melodramas and ghost stories that little tortoiseshell cats react violently to the sight of corpses. In real life I'm afraid it isn't so. For a cat to get into that alarming state there has to be some much livelier stimulus. A dog was one possibility; but a dog would have made itself heard. So how about another cat? The family were fond of cats, I'd heard, so very likely they owned one. And it wouldn't have been difficult for Doyle to stuff the wretched creature through one of the little windows . . . He'd noticed the blood on the panel, you see—which of course had been smeared there by the cat—and worked it out that if the cat were disposed of, that panel could be made the foundation for a murder charge.

"Naturally, he'd have buried the cat, later. But while he was telephoning the police, I was out looking for the poor thing, which eventually I found in the bushes, near the foot of the tower, where it had crawled to die. A white Siamese it was: no blood on its paws, but a big splotch, acquired obviously at the very moment of Copping's death, on its flank."

"So Copping did it himself," said the fair-haired girl who had spoken before. "What a sell . . ." She hesitated, and then suddenly her eyes grew shrewd. *"Or did he?* The fact that this man Doyle tried to incriminate his wife doesn't necessarily mean that she wasn't guilty, does it?"

"Clever girl." Fen smiled at her. "Actually, it wasn't until twelve weeks later that the servant the police had suborned caught Isobel burning the blood-stained frock she'd worn to kill her father . . . But better late than never. And it makes a good ending, don't you think? Nice to know that these old family traditions die so hard."

THE LION'S TOOTH

IT LAY EMBEDDED in crudely wrought silver, with a surround of big lustreless semi-precious stones; graven on the reverse of the silver was an outline which Fen recognized as the ichthys, pass-sign of primitive Christianity.

"Naturally, one thinks of Androcles," said the reverend mother. "Or if not of him specially, then of the many other early Christians who faced the lions in the arena." She paused, then added: "This, you know, is the convent's only relic. Apparently it is also our only clue."

She stooped to replace it in the sacristy cupboard; and Fen, while he waited, thought of frail old Sister St Jude, whose only intelligible words, since they had found her had been "The tooth of a lion!", and again—urgently, repeatedly—"The tooth of a lion!"

He thought, too, of the eleven-year-old girl who had been kidnapped and of her father who had obstinately refused to divulge to the police the medium through which the ransom was to be paid, for fear that in trying to catch the kidnapper they would blunder and bring about the death of his only child. He would rather pay, he had said; and from this decision he was in no way to be moved . . .

It had been the reverend mother who had insisted on consult-ing Fen; but following her now, as she led the way back to her office, he doubted if there was much he could do. The available facts were altogether too arid and too few. Thus: Francis Merrill was middle-aged, a widower and a wealthy business-man. Two weeks ago, immediately after Christmas, he had gone off to the Continent, leaving his daughter Mary, at her own special request, to the care of the sisters. During the mornings Mary had helped the sisters with their chores. But in the afternoons, with the reverend mother's encouragement, she would usually go out and ramble round the countryside.

On most of these outings Mary Merrill was accompanied, for a short distance, by Sister St Jude. Sister St Jude was ailing; the doctors, however, had decreed that she must get plenty of fresh air, so even through the recent long weeks of frost and ice she had continued to issue forth, well wrapped up, and spend an hour or two each afternoon on a sheltered seat near the summit of the small hill at the convent's back. It had been Mary Merrill's habit to see her settled there and then to wander off on her own.

Until, this last Tuesday, a search-party of the sisters had come upon Sister St Jude sprawled near her accustomed seat with concussion of the brain.

Mary Merrill had not come home that night. The reverend mother had, of course, immediately notified the police; and Francis Merrill, hastening back from Italy, had found a ransom note awaiting him.

To all intents and purposes, that was all; the police, it seemed, had so far achieved precisely nothing. If only—Fen reflected—if *only* one knew more about the *girl herself*: for instance, where she was likely to have gone, and what she was likely to have done, on these rambles of hers. But Francis Merrill had refused even to meet Fen; and the reverend mother had been unable to produce any information about Mary more specific and instructive than the statement that she had been a friendly, trusting, *ordinary* sort of child . . .

"I suppose," said Fen, collapsing into a chair, "that it's quite certain Sister St Jude has never said anything comprehensible *other* than this phrase about the lion's tooth?"

"Absolutely certain, I am afraid," the reverend mother replied. "Apart from a few—a few sounds which may conceivably have been French words, she has not yet been able—"

"*French* words?"

"Yes. I should have mentioned, perhaps, that Sister St Jude is a Frenchwoman."

"I see," said Fen slowly. "I see. . . . Tell me, did she—does she, I mean—speak English at all fluently?"

"Not very fluently, no. She has only been over here a matter of nine months or so. Her vocabulary, for instance, is still rather limited . . ." The reverend mother hesitated. "Perhaps you are thinking that the phrase about the lion's tooth may have been mis-heard. But she has used it many times, in the presence of many of us—including Sister Bartholomew, who is another

Frenchwoman—and we have none of us ever had the least doubt about what the words were."

"Not mis-heard," said Fen pensively. "But misinterpreted, perhaps . . ." Looking up, the reverend mother saw that he was on his feet again. "Reverend Mother, I have an idea," he went on. "Or an inkling, rather. At present I don't at all see how it *applies*. But none the less, I think that if you'll excuse me, I'll go now and take a look at the place where Sister St Jude was attacked. There's a certain object to be looked for there, which the police may well have found, but decided to ignore."

"What kind of object?" the reverend mother asked.

And Fen smiled at her. "Yellow," he said. "Something yellow."

No prolonged search was needed; there the thing lay, in full view of everyone, as plain as the nose on a policeman's face. In a mood of complacency which the reverend mother could hardly have approved, Fen pocketed it, climbed the remaining distance to the top of the little hill, and looked around him. The complacency waned somewhat; from this vantage-point he could see buildings galore. Still, with any luck at all. . . .

The gods were with him that day; within three hours—three hours of peering over hedges, and of surreptitious trespassing in other people's gardens—he located the particular house he sought. A glance at the local directory, a rapid but rewarding contact with the child population of a neighbouring village, and by six o'clock he was ready for action.

The man who answered the knock on the front door was grey-haired, weedy, nervous-seeming; while not unprepossessing, he yet had something of a hungry look. "Mr Jones?" said Fen, pushing him back into his own hall before he had time to realize what was happening, and without waiting for a reply, added: "I've come for the child."

"The child?" Mr Jones looked blank. "There's no child here. I'm afraid you've got the wrong house."

"Indeed I haven't," said Fen confidently. And even as he spoke, the thin, high scream of a young girl welled up from somewhere on the premises, followed by incoherent, sobbing appeals for help. Fen noted the particular door to which pallid Mr Jones's eyes immediately turned: an interesting door, in that it lay well away from the direction whence the scream had come . . .

"Yes, we'll go through there, I think," said Fen pleasantly; and now there was an automatic pistol in his hand. "It leads to the cellar, I expect. And since I'm not at all fond of men who try to smash in the skulls of helpless old nuns, you may rely on my shooting you without the slightest hesitation or compunction if you make a single false move."

Later, when Mr Jones had been taken away by the police, and Mary Merrill, hysterical but otherwise not much harmed, restored to her father, Fen went round to the back garden, where he found an engaging female urchin wandering about eating a large bar of chocolate cream.

"That was jolly good," he told her, handing over the promised ten-shilling note. "When you grow up, you ought to go on the stage."

She grinned at him. "Some scream, mister, eh?" she said.

"Some scream," Fen agreed.

And: "It's obvious," he said to the reverend mother over lunch next day, "that Mary Merrill made friends with Jones soon after she came here, and got into the way of visiting him pretty well every afternoon. No harm in that. But then he found out who her father was and began envisaging the possibility of making some easy money.

"What actually *happened,* I understand, is that Mary, on that last visit, took fright at something odd and constrained in his attitude to her, and succeeded in slipping away while his back was turned. Whereupon he very stupidly followed her (in his car, except for the last bit) and tried to grab her when she was already quite close to home.

"She eluded him again, and ran to Sister St Jude for protection. But by that time Jones had gone too far for retreat to be practicable or safe; so he ran after her, struck Sister St Jude down with his stick, and this time really did succeed in capturing Mary, knocking her out, and so getting her back to his house.

"Whether the dandelion part of it belongs to that particular afternoon, or to some previous one, one doesn't know, but whichever it was, Sister St Jude clearly *noticed* the flower and equally clearly realized, even in her illness and delirium, that it provided a clue to——"

"Wait, please," the reverend mother implored him faintly. "Did I hear you say 'dandelion'?"

And Fen nodded. "Yes, dandelion. English corruption of the French dent-de-lion—which of course means a lion's tooth. But Sister St Jude's vocabulary was limited: *she* didn't know the English name for it. Therefore, she translated it literally, forgetting altogether the existence of that confusing, but irrelevant, relic of yours——

"Well, I ask you: a dandelion, in January, after weeks of hard frost! But Mary Merrill had managed to find one; had picked it and then perhaps pushed it into a button-hole of her frock. As every gardener knows, dandelions are prolific and hardy brutes; but in view of the recent weather, this particular dandelion could really *only* have come from a weed in a hot-house within an hour's walk from here. As soon as I saw Jones's, I was certain it was the right one."

The reverend mother looked at him. "You were, were you?" she said.

"Well, no, actually I wasn't certain at all," Fen admitted. "But I thought that the luck I'd had up to then would probably hold, and I was tired of tramping about, and anyway I haven't the slightest objection to terrorizing innocent householders so long as it's in a good cause . . . may I smoke?"

GLADSTONE'S CANDLESTICK

GINA MITCHELL, sitting very upright on the edge of her chair, accepted a cigarette, lit it, looked her tutor defiantly in the eye, and announced without preliminary: "I am *not* a thief. All the evidence is against me, I'll admit that, but none the less it *wasn't* me, really it wasn't me, and what I want is for you to——"

"Steady," said Fen. "Take it easy, and don't try to bully me, please." But then he smiled; for he liked the girl, and clearly her distress was genuine. "Start at the beginning," he suggested.

"Thanks," she said, trying to speak lightly, and failing. "Thanks. I was hoping you might be willing to listen, and—well, anyway, here's what happened . . ."

Gina had only two living relatives, she said: her grandfather, Lord Stretham, who lived at Horton Manor, a few miles the other side of Abingdon; and her cousin, Humphrey Linster. Three months previously, these two had gone off together on a long cruise, in an attempt to bolster up Lord Stretham's failing health.

The project had failed, however: Lord Stretham had returned to Horton Manor three days ago in an ambulance, bedridden. And although in himself he remained reasonably cheerful, there was no certainty that he would last out the year.

On their return, the travellers had found Gina waiting for them at the house. She had wanted to do a drawing of an Adam fireplace in one of the rooms. Sketching, her hobby, now and again earned her a little pocket-money, and there was a series to be completed by the end of the week . . .

"There are actually two Adam rooms in the manor," she told Fen. "They're connected, end to end; and a year ago grandfather had them locked up, because they weren't being used enough. He was quite willing to let me have the key—incidentally, he'd taken the key with him on the cruise—and also he asked me to stay a couple of nights, and of course I said I'd be glad to.

"After I'd seen them settled in I duly went off and did my drawing. As grandfather had warned me, it was very dusty and musty in there, after being shut up for so long. Oh, and I should explain that it was the fireplace in the first of the two rooms that I was interested in; I never went into the further room at all.

"When I'd finished, I closed up the shutters again, and locked the door carefully after me. But having done that, I unluckily forgot, for the time being, to return the key. It stayed with me till after lunch the following day—yesterday, that is. Unfortunately, I'm quite sure that no one had the chance to 'borrow' it from me during the time it was in my possession.

"The next thing that happened was that an acquaintance of grandfather's, a man called Henry Challis, dropped in unexpectedly for lunch (this is still yesterday I'm speaking of). And *he* wanted to look at the Adam rooms.

"Grandfather asked my cousin Humphrey to show them to him after lunch, and told him to be sure not to miss the big eighteenth-century musical-box in the first room, and in the second, the pair of hideous great ornate gold candlesticks which someone had given to Gladstone in 1868 and Gladstone had hurriedly passed on to my great-great-grandfather; their gold made them worth about £400 apiece, grandfather said, but aesthetically they were quite monstrous, of course.

"So presently Humphrey and this man Challis came to me for the key to the rooms, which I still had, and they went off on their tour of inspection . . . Challis"—Gina grimaced—"well, I'm afraid there's no possible chance of his having been in collusion with Humphrey; nor of his having told lies for any other reason.

"Anyway, in they went, and Humphrey opened the shutters in the first room and left Challis playing with the musical-box there while he went on to let some light in on the further room. After a bit Challis joined him, and they saw straight away that one of the candlesticks was missing.

"Humphrey muttered that they ought both to be there, because they had been when he and grandfather had been in the rooms just before they set off on the cruise. They should have been standing one at each end of the mantelpiece, he said: but now, only too obviously, the left-hand one had vanished.

"When Challis heard this, he fetched a chair and got up on it—that particular mantelpiece is above eye-level—to have a closer look. And there he saw the—imprint, I suppose you'd call it, of the candlestick's base: a clean, distinctively shaped patch without any dust on it worth speaking of.

"They called Holmes, the manservant, and the three of them searched the room. No candlestick. The windows, as well as being shuttered, were nailed, and quite evidently neither they, nor the expensive lock on the door leading to the rest of the house, had been tampered with in any way; I checked that myself, before I left.

"As to Challis or Humphrey or Holmes having the wretched thing hidden on their—on their persons, the mere size of it put that possibility completely out of court."

Gina flushed slightly. "So you see the situation that that left me in. Grandfather wouldn't even listen to me. He just turned his head away and said there was no point in labouring the matter, but that in the circumstances I might feel happier if I didn't remain in his house. So by dinner-time I'd packed up and left . . .

"There's no question of prosecution, of course," said Gina in conclusion. "But just the same, Professor Fen, *I did not steal that candlestick.*"

For a while Fen pondered. Then he said: "Assuming that you *are* innocent, and that the key couldn't have been borrowed from you while it was in your possession, and that Challis is honest—well, that really leaves only two possibilities, doesn't it? Your grandfather or your cousin."

"Yes, but how?"

"Oh, as to how . . ." Fen chuckled. "The 'how' is quite simple, I should say—and you don't have to postulate any nonsense about duplicate keys in order to arrive at it, either."

Then he frowned. "Proof, though . . . Ah well, there's at least a 50–50 chance, I imagine. What I'll do is go and see your grandfather about it: I do know him slightly. . . .

"And then—let's see, we've got a tutorial together in about a week's time, haven't we? With any luck at all, I'll have some news for you then."

It was Gina, radiant, who produced the first piece of news at their next meeting after the week had elapsed. "A letter this morning from grandfather," she exulted. "Very apologetic, and will I please forgive him and go and visit him again as soon as I possibly can. But he doesn't explain *why*, and——"

"The 'why', I fancy," said Fen, "is a letter he had from me, enclosing an authoritative laboratory report . . . Incidentally, I too have had an apology from him. He was pretty chilly when I went to see him, although he allowed me to do what I wanted (and also unwittingly gave me the chance to pay an unauthorized visit to a certain bedroom). Your cousin Humphrey, I'm afraid, will now be in just as great disfavour as you were; only *he* deserves it."

Gina nodded soberly. "I thought it must be Humphrey," she said. "But, honestly, I still can't understand how he managed it."

Fen snorted. "You take things too much for granted," he said. "And of course, the thing you were taking too much for granted in this instance was that nice clean outline left by the base of the candlestick in the surrounding dust.

"Obviously—there being, apart from the duplicate-key hypothesis, no other conceivable explanation—obviously cousin Humphrey stole the candlestick *before* he and his grandfather went off on their cruise; intending, I imagine, to pawn it for ready money, and later to redeem and replace it . . .

"It must have come as a nasty shock to him when immediately on his return not one person but two were given the entrée to those rooms which only he and his grandfather had visited since they were shut up. You were a tolerable risk, since you were concerned only with the first of the two rooms—not with the one where the candlesticks were. But Challis was a different matter.

"Challis's attention had been specially drawn to the candlesticks, so that the disappearance of one of them was bound to be discovered—with the dust on the mantelpiece indicating plainly that it had been gone a good long time . . .

"Well, you'll have realized by now what Humphrey did. While Challis fooled about with the musical-box in the first room, Humphrey went on into the second; and there had sufficient time to wipe the end of the mantelpiece where the stolen candlestick had stood; transfer to the cleared area the second (identical) candlestick; puff a layer of dust round it, with the help of his shaving-powder puffer, loaded in readiness with raw material from the vacuum-cleaner; and then, leaving a fine, sharp imprint, replace the remaining candlestick in its proper position.

"I myself found the puffer on my surreptitious visit to your cousin's bedroom. By then he'd had time to wash it out and refill it with shaving powder; but at least it was *there*—and also I was able to make a note of the brand of shaving-powder he used. . . .

THE MAN WHO LOST HIS HEAD

LONDON CLUBS ARE not usually much frequented in the earlier hours of the day; so that when Sir Gerald McComas entered the main smoking-room of the United University shortly after 8.30 that sultry June morning, he found Gervase Fen in sole occupation. The two men were only slightly acquainted, and Fen was consequently a shade surprised when the millionaire art collector came over and settled down beside him.

Presently, however, he launched with perceptible effort into an appeal for help. It had to be someone he *knew*, he said; on the other hand, it mustn't be anyone he knew *too well*—else the appearance, and perhaps also the substance, of impartiality would be lacking.

"You see, sir, the fact is"—Sir Gerald explained, at long last reaching the nub of the matter—"the fact is that I'm rather afraid my daughter's fiancé may have—well, to put it bluntly, may have stolen something from me."

And then it all came pouring out.

Jane McComas had got herself engaged, it seemed, to a fledgling barrister by the name of Brian Ainsworth: a good enough fellow, though perhaps not quite the match for Jane that Sir Gerald himself would have chosen . . . Anyway, for the past few days this young man had been staying at the McComas house in Lowndes Square.

Yesterday afternoon he had taken Jane out to a cocktail party, from which they had returned only just in time to dress for dinner. And although Sir Gerald hated saying this, Ainsworth really had had several drinks too many.

When Sir Gerald mildly remonstrated as the young man reached a fourth time for the brandy decanter, a quarrel had flared up which had culminated in Ainsworth's losing his temper completely and rushing out of the house into the night.

Unluckily, however, his headlong departure had carried him straight into the arms of a patrolling constable, whom in his anger he had unwisely tried to push aside; whereupon the constable

"The dust surrounding the supposed imprint of the stolen candlestick—which happily he hadn't a chance to tamper with —was thereupon sent by me, along with a sample from elsewhere on the mantlepiece, to a laboratory. The two lots proved to be substantially different—which unless one of them had been faked was a scientific impossibility. And to clinch it, identifiable grains of shaving-powder were found in the first sample."

Fen smiled. "Satisfied?" he asked.

had promptly arrested him for being drunk and disorderly.

"So he spent last night in a cell," said Sir Gerald, "and this morning they'll be hauling him up in front of a magistrate. That doesn't matter, though; the really *serious* thing is that when I went back indoors after all this rumpus, I found that a small but valuable Leonardo drawing, a 'Head of a man', had vanished from a portfolio in my study.

"Now, the point is this. I'd last looked at that drawing shortly after lunch-time, and subsequent to that there were only two occasions when the study wasn't either (a) well locked up or (b) occupied by me.

"The first of these occasions was during the afternoon, when I gave Jane the key so that she could fetch a book she wanted; and if you're thinking that perhaps she didn't lock up properly afterwards you can put that out of your mind, because as it happens I went along to the study myself, and settled down there, before Jane left it. I've checked with her, and she's quite certain that no one except herself can have entered the room during the five minutes when she had possession of the key.

"Which leaves the second occasion. The study's the most comfortable room in the house to lounge in, so after dinner I had our coffee and our drinks taken there. And that's how it happened that for a minute or so young Ainsworth was left alone with the portfolio: you see, Jane, who was telephoning somebody from the hall, called me out to ask me some question about our plans for the next few days; and of course I never dreamed . . .

"Well, damn it!" said Sir Gerald unhappily. "I mean, partiality aside, it really is quite inconceivable to me that *Jane* can be the thief: the girl knows perfectly well that I'd gladly give her any amount of money if she wanted it, and no questions asked: for that matter, I'd willingly give her the drawing itself.

"And I dare say you see what I've been driving at: unless Ainsworth's managed to jettison the drawing—which with police all round him would be a madly risky thing to attempt—he's bound to have it still on him this morning when they let him go free . . . Yes, yes, I know they make people turn out their pockets before they're shoved into the cells. But they don't bother to do *more* than that—not with a man of Ainsworth's class, on a drunk charge. Therefore, what I'm aiming at is to catch Ainsworth as soon as he comes out, take him to one of my offices near by, and—well, and ask him to agree to being searched."

Fen stared. "I should hardly imagine," he said presently, "that Ainsworth is going to like *that* suggestion very much."

"No, of course he's not." Sir Gerald's embarrassment was causing him to positively wriggle in his chair. "But you see the position I'm in. I don't care tuppence about the wretched drawing; to save a scandal he can have that, and welcome. But if he really is a thief, then it's essential I prove it to Jane before she goes off and elopes with him, or some other damn silly thing.

"What I shall actually say to him is that if he doesn't agree to this . . . this admittedly very distasteful expedient, I shall simply hand him over straight away to the police and leave them to deal with the affair."

"H'm," said Fen. "I should have thought, you know, that you had pretty conclusive evidence against him already."

"Jane insists that I must be mistaken," said Sir Gerald. "About not having left the study unlocked, I mean. Also I think that perhaps she suspects . . . no, never mind that. The important thing is that although she's terribly angry about this scheme of mine, she has in fact agreed to come along. And the question now is, would you be prepared to come along, too, and see fair play?"

Fen considered the prospect and found it not much to his liking. At the same time, the situation had possibilities which Sir Gerald either had not realized or else had not thought fit to specify; and in the latter event it was Fen's positive *duty* to go. . . .

The court proceedings—the charge, the evidence, the expected fine—passed without incident. Emerging from the court-room, Ainsworth found the little group of three awaiting him in the corridor outside; and, incongruous in his dinner jacket, listened in silence while Sir Gerald brusquely outlined the situation and made his proposal. Then he turned to Jane.

"Do *you* want me to submit to this?" he asked.

Jane McComas's auburn hair gleamed in the weak sunlight as she raised her head to look steadily at him. "No," she breathed. "No darling, *no*. Call his bluff. Let him tell the police. You haven't got anything to be afraid of."

"No?" Ainsworth raised his eyebrows. "Not even the scandal?

I'm sorry, my dear, but I'm afraid that if I'm going to go on being a barrister, I simply *must* choose the discreeter alternative of the two . . ."

And with that he moved off abruptly. "Let's get it over with," he said, "shall we?"

As things turned out, it was Fen who actually found the drawing. The tacks holding down the insole of Ainsworth's left shoe had been rooted up, and the folded paper inserted beneath; the insole had then been pressed back into place.

"So that," said Sir Gerald heavily, "is that." And he went into the adjoining room to fetch Jane. Fen, however, remained with Ainsworth; and after a little reflection said:

"Ainsworth, just *when* did you hide this drawing in the shoe?"

The young man looked up briefly, and Fen was interested to note that he hesitated perceptibly before replying. "If you must know," he said, "I had it under my shirt to start with, and then put it into the shoe in my cell during the night. Any more questions?"

Fen considered. "Yes, two, I think. And here's the first of them. Is Jane McComas fond of her father, would you say?"

Ainsworth seemed momentarily bewildered by this. "Not really very fond, no," he said. "But——"

"Thanks. And the other thing I want to know is whether, from start to finish, there was any occasion apart from your . . . your pernoctation in the cell when the drawing could have been transferred to the shoe." Fen waited. "Well? Was there?"

After a bursting pause: "No," said Ainsworth expressionlessly. "No. As a matter of fact there wasn't."

"You realize I can check that statement?"

And suddenly, Ainsworth smiled, and in an altered tone said:

"All right then, go ahead." It was as though a great weight had been lifted from him. "Go ahead and check it. Only . . . only don't do anything too drastic about the result, will you? I mean, if we could just talk it over . . ."

"We will," Fen assured him; and with that left the building and took a cab to New Scotland Yard, where, through the good offices of his friend Detective Inspector Humbleby, he was able in due course to confirm what he had suspected; that in fact there had been no other occasion when Ainsworth could possibly have put the portrait into the shoe . . .

*   *   *

"You're an ass, though," he told Ainsworth that evening in the bar where they had arranged to meet. "A chivalrous ass, of course; but still an ass."

"Chivalrous?" Ainsworth shook his head. "Hardly that. The point was that although I never much liked the old boy, I had to give him credit for being fond of his daughter; and it would have pretty well shattered him to find out what she's done . . . *You* haven't told him, have you?"

"Not my business," said Fen, "but am I to take it that you're proposing to let Sir Gerald go on imagining you're guilty? I don't myself see the slightest reason why you should."

"There is a reason, though." Ainsworth spoke very soberly. "I was carrying on with another girl, you see, while I was still engaged to Jane. Not nice—I owe them something for that. Of course, I was *intending* to break off the engagement; but when Jane did eventually find out about the other girl, the fat really was in the fire.

"In those circumstances, merely breaking with me must have seemed to her to be a most inadequate punishment; so she worked out a clever little plan to try to ruin me professionally as well, by making me out to be a thief . . ."

"But how did you know it was the girl who was trying to frame you, rather than the father?"

"Ah, well, you see, it was her, not him, that I saw coming out of my bedroom yesterday afternoon with one of those little tools you use for prising up tacks. She didn't know I'd seen her—and naturally I myself thought nothing of it, at the time. It was only when the drawing turned up in my shoe that I put two and two together and decided on my self-sacrificing act." Ainsworth grinned. "Thank the Lord you were around to puncture it . . . Incidentally, why *do* they take one's shoes away when they lock one up?"

"It's really only the laces," Fen explained, "that they're *supposed* to take; the idea is that if the laces are left with you you may upset the routine by deciding to hang yourself during the night. Your lie in answer to my question was an unavoidable one, of course, in view of the fact that there wasn't any other time when you could have put the drawing in the shoe; though I supposed that you'd simply refuse to say anything at all."

"No, I didn't dare try that. You obviously had something

on your mind, and I was afraid that obstinate silence, on an apparently trivial point, would make you even more suspicious than you already were."

Ainsworth sighed. "Well, well, I've been several sorts of a fool, but it's all over now. Jane's plan *could* have succeeded, you know, if I hadn't taken it into my head to try to swipe that policeman . . ."

And Fen chuckled. "Yes," he said. "You may thank your lucky stars that Sir Gerald McComas wasn't the only person, in Lowndes Square that evening, who lost his head."

THE TWO SISTERS

"MY DEAR BOY"—his aunt had written—"certainly you may use the cottage while I am in France. The only condition I make is that you bring your own china: my Spode really is irreplaceable . . . My housekeeper, Mrs Blench, has agreed to stay on and look after you, and, apart from her deafness (you have to write everything down for her, I am afraid), you will find her an excellent servant.

"I should warn you, however, that she has a disreputable sister, called Bessie, who is always pestering her for money, and who is not to be encouraged on any account. Unfortunately, Mrs Blench insists on keeping large sums in the house (she is the stupid sort of woman that distrusts banks), so please see to it that the doors and windows are properly fastened at nights.

"You will find it rather a lonely spot, but no doubt that will be an advantage to you in your convalescence, since I understand that in these cases peace and quiet are essential. You should turn left off the Southampton road at . . ."

There followed directions, with a map.

And "lonely" was right, Percy Wyndham reflected as his car ground to a halt on the short gravel drive; it was three miles since he had passed the last dwelling-place.

He did not repine, however. This trim little cottage, surrounded on all sides by the great oaks and beeches of the New Forest, was just the thing for a man recovering from a nervous breakdown. Unloading the crate which held his utility china he trudged with it up to the front door.

This was ajar; and just inside it, on the polished floor, lay a small, light-weight, wholly lethal Persian mat. Wyndham noted the first fact but not, unfortunately for him, the second. His entrance consequently took the form of a long, graceless skid—during which he just had time to take in the fact that the housekeeper, with her back to him, was impassively dusting the hall-stand.

She was small, greying, middle-aged, neat, and, above all,

respectable; her only noticeable characteristic was her voice, which had a flat, uninflected quality—the result, undoubtedly, of long years of deafness.

But it was plain that Mrs Blench was going to be a very satisfactory servant. Having to write things down for her was a nuisance, of course: but she had already suggested that a single word would do.

Above all, she was tranquil. The only sign of anxiety that she had manifested had been when Wyndham presented her with a laboured narrative explaining that he was suffering from insomnia, that even with the aid of drugs he was seldom able to sleep more than three hours or so after going to bed, and that therefore she must not alarm herself and think of burglars if she heard him moving about—going out for a stroll in the garden, perhaps—during the night.

Noting her uneasiness, he added a codicil to the effect that he would not on any account leave the cottage unlocked, or if unlocked, unwatched during the dark hours, and this seemed to reassure her.

Probably her chief worry in this connection was sister Bessie. When Wyndham looked into the kitchen later that evening, his eye was caught by a woman's handkerchief, lipstick stained, which lay on the dresser, and which Mrs Blench, following his glance, thrust into her pocket with a murmured apology. Mrs Blench wore no make-up of any kind; it was to be presumed therefore, that Bessie had taken advantage of the gap between his aunt's departure and his own arrival to pay a visit.

In accordance as much with his own inclination as with his aunt's instructions, Wyndham locked up carefully that night; then, having undressed, swallowed a sleeping-pill and presently contrived to drop off. This time, however, his slumber lasted little more than an hour and he knew from experience that it was useless to try to recapture it once it had gone. Cursing, he sat up in bed and groped for a cigarette. Outside, it was a still night; and——

But was it so still? Just what was that rustling and trampling in the garden?

Thoroughly disquieted, Wyndham got out of bed and went to the window; and what he saw caused him to fling it open, calling out.

At the bottom of the garden, where there was a gap giving access to the forest proper, lit by a gibbous moon but barred with shadow, two indistinct figures struggled and swayed. Even as Wyndham watched, one of them seemed to break away and the other to fall . . . Bedroom slippers; staircase; and so out through the unbolted back door.

Thus it was that he came to Mrs Blench, where she lay fully dressed, panting and exhausted, beside the rubbish-heap. But her assailant was gone; and when he moved to follow, Mrs Blench caught at him and held him, fiercely.

"I told her I knew about this Bessie creature," said Wyndham after lunch next day, remembering the serio-comic "dialogue" which had followed the previous night's events, "and she didn't attempt to deny that that was who it had been. Police, I said—wrote, rather. But no, she wasn't bringing the police into it, not to set them on to her own flesh and blood. *I* don't know what to do. It's obvious the sister's lurking about somewhere in this neighbourhood. And although it's possible I've scared her off for good, I shouldn't like to bank on it."

Gervase Fen, who had dropped in on his way back from Southampton to London, and who had been told the whole story in detail, said thoughtfully: "No, I don't suppose you've seen the end of it yet . . . Have you been out today at all?"

"Not so far."

"Good. I shouldn't, if I were you. Stay in the house—or the garden—and keep an eye on things. Look here, could you put me up for the night? I know you're not in the mood for visitors, but——"

"I'd be glad to," said Wyndham, sincerely. "You think something more is going to happen tonight, do you?"

"Yes. We're not going to face it alone, either. If you'll excuse me for an hour or so, I'll drive into Lyndhurst and have a word with the inspector there."

With the result that that night, a decent interval after having apparently retired to bed, two male figures might have been seen descending shakily from their bedroom windows. "We'll lay our ambush well away from the house," Fen had said; and in fact they were some distance into the forest before they came to their rendezvous with the police. For more than an hour the party waited vainly, then at long last came footsteps—

but moving *away* from the direction of the cottage, Wyndham noticed, not towards it. For a moment this perplexed him— until he realized that this must be Mrs Blench, not Bessie; that Mrs Blench was boldly (or foolhardily) seeking her sister out in order to——

That was when the figure actually came into view. In the leaf-filtered moonlight it had a curiously humped look, and it was moving slowly, apparently with effort . . . It came closer. It was there. And suddenly the powerful beam of the inspector's torch was shining on Mrs Blench's face, and on the thing that she carried . . .

He said: "Bessie Moulford, I arrest you for the murder of your sister Charlotte Blench, and I have to warn you that anything you say may be taken down and used in evidence at your trial."

"Yes," said Fen later, over the coffee which Wyndham had brewed, "Bessie must have strangled her sister almost immediately before your arrival—presumably somewhere in the house and presumably for the sake of the money Mrs Blench kept there.

"Your appearance cut off her retreat. So as an emergency measure she impersonated Mrs Blench; and during the night attempted to remove the body. The 'grappling' you saw in the garden was simply a small, middle-aged woman trying to cope with a heavy corpse—and of course the handkerchief with lip-stick on it had precisely the opposite significance to what you imagined."

Wyndham nodded. "I see. When she realized I was awake, she just had time to shove the body out of the way, somewhere near by, before I actually left the house. No wonder she didn't want me to start looking around—and, incidentally, no wonder she was so upset when she heard I suffered from insomnia!"

"And of course *after* you'd interrupted her first attempt," Fen added, "there was no chance for her to do anything further about the body, with any safety, before tonight. I located it, as you'll have guessed, before I went to the police; but it was essential, they thought, to catch her in the act of moving it again."

"What did I miss?" Wyndham asked.

"Oh, the significance of your fall, when you smashed the china."

"But she *didn't* react to that."

"Quite," said Fen. "That was how I realized she was sham-ming deafness—wasn't, in fact, what she pretended to be. A genuinely deaf person would have felt the vibration of that heavy fall, conducted through the floor and walls, and would have turned at once."

OUTRAGE IN STEPNEY

BY THE CLOSE of Herr Dietrich's peroration Gervase Fen had become decidedly restive. The hall was chilly and airless, the first delightful impact of Communism's musty Victorian-sounding zoological similes—"Fascist jackal", "Capitalist leeches"—had grown stale with repetition, and in general Fen felt that he had had enough of political slumming to last him for quite some time to come. He waited while an inflammatory question about the American president was asked and lengthily answered —Eisenhower, it seemed (pronounced by Herr Dietrich "Eisss-enhoer" with all the sibilance of extreme hatred) was directly responsible, along with the vultures of Wall Street, for Germany's continued partition—and then nudged his companion and crept out. In the streets, breathing soot-laden Stepney air, he lit a cigarette. And presently the other—whose name was Campbell and who belonged to Scotland Yard's Special Branch—joined him there.

"Well, thanks for bringing me," said Fen. "Do you have to go back?"

Campbell shook his head. "No, I don't think it's necessary. Apart from riots with Fascists, nothing interesting ever happens at these public do's. What did you think of Dietrich?"

Fen paused a moment before replying. Then he said slowly: "I suppose that really *was* Dietrich?"

Campbell stared. "Good heavens, yes. He's far too well-known, and far too distinctive-looking, for them to dream of trying to substitute anyone else. Anyway, why should they? From the point of view of the Stepney Communist Party, he's a great catch."

"Yes, I suppose so . . . The sort of man," Fen added pensively, "who would have a lot of useful information to give us about what's going on in East Berlin."

"Would but won't," said Campbell. "You can take it as read that he'll be kept surrounded by watchful comrades the whole time he's over here. Since Petrov, they've been very cagey about that sort of thing. So that even if Dietrich did feel inclined to ask for asylum, he'd have to do a tricky escaping act first . . . Not," Campbell went on, probing delicately, "that we have any reason to suppose——"

"Nothing that would convince your superiors, no," said Fen with a grin. "Just the same, I should like to know where Dietrich and his friends are likely to go when the meeting's over."

Campbell regarded him with suspicion. "Look here, you be careful," he said. "Some of these people are genuinely dangerous. If you're thinking of trying to strike up an acquaintance——"

"I am not," said Fen truthfully. "I'm curious, that's all. How do the comrades relax? Will they go to a pub, I mean, or——"

"They'll probably go to that pub over there." Campbell pointed across the road. "The Grapes."

"Good. I can do with a drink. And don't you worry about me. I'm quite capable of looking after myself."

Campbell contemplated him for a moment, then nodded. "Yes," he said. "I believe you are. Just don't start heiling Mosley when you're in The Grapes, that's all. The clients don't much like that sort of thing." He smiled and waved and went.

Fen had no intention of heiling Mosley, in The Grapes or anywhere else. He bought beer and settled down by the bar to read the evening paper, with the Light Programme burbling innocuously at his elbow; and after half an hour or so was rewarded by the arrival of Dietrich with three English comrades—a young fanatical-looking one, an older and decidedly tough one, and a clerkly fellow in rimless glasses. They carried their drinks to a table in the corner, and Fen began taking serious stock of the situation.

It was unpromising, he found. Dietrich was obviously being closely watched, and it was clear that conversational overtures from a stranger such as Fen would arouse instant suspicion. Some communication with Dietrich there plainly must be, however, if anything were to be accomplished. As to how——

". . . opens our programme of 'Music for the Multitude'," said the radio, "with that rousing . . ."

At which Fen sat upright abruptly on his stool, and for the first time that evening favoured the Light Programme with the whole of his attention. For he had recognized the announcer's voice. By one of those coincidences which are so much commoner in life than in fiction, this particular announcer was an ex-pupil of Fen's. Fen knew, moreover, that he had quarrelled with the BBC and was leaving them quite shortly. And that being so——

There was a telephone-box a short way along the road. Fen left the bar, and after a rapid reconnaissance of the back of the inn's premises, made two calls.

At The Grapes, when he returned there, he was gratified to find everything as before. He resumed his position at the back, and presently, when the second item of "Music for the Multitude" had reached its tawdry conclusion, stretched out his hand, as if idly, to twist the radio's volume control.

"We come now," said the announcer, "to a popular march based on the old German folk-tune 'Der hohe Herr am Barwird Ihnen winken: dann, deutscher Kamerad, gehen Sie bitte sofort in die Herren'. Ladies and gentlemen—'Anchors Aweigh'."

A great splurge of brass and cymbals filled the room. At a glare from the landlord Fen hurriedly turned the volume down again and went back to his paper. Perhaps ten minutes later, a very large, very drunk young man appeared and demanded a double whisky. With an air of great self-approval, he drank about half of this. Then all at once his expression altered; he mumbled something; holding a hand to his mouth, he made hurriedly for one of the doors at the back.

"There's another of them can't take it," said Fen to the landlord. The landlord nodded, and with mournful emphasis Fen nodded back.

Dietrich got to his feet. Now he was heading for the door the young man had disappeared through. The tough middle-aged comrade was following, while the younger one slipped out into the street—no doubt with a view to stationing himself strategically under the relevant window. Fen finished his drink and left. In the narrowing deserted street behind The Grapes he was in time to see a car's tail-light vanishing. The youthful comrade, though unlikely to recover consciousness for some minutes, was not seriously injured, Fen thought. He went and found himself a taxi.

"Most irregular," said Sir Somebody two hours later, in an office of the Special Branch whose whereabouts is not known to the general public. "Two respected citizens of Stepney with great stunning bruises on the backs of their heads, and no trace of miscreants . . ."

"Undergraduates, perhaps," Fen suggested. "For instance, I happen to know that a couple of pupils of mine are in London at the moment——"

"No, they'll never be caught." Sir Somebody was firm. "Not a chance of it, I'm afraid. As to this business of kidnapping an important personage from East Berlin . . . well, really . . ."

Herr Dietrich grinned all over his broad, florid face. "Such a very good plan," he murmured. "At the first, you realize, I am a little surprised that it is carried out by amateurs. But then I understand that most probably my hint is too slight to be acted on by your—what do you call it? by your big brass. I am surrounded all the time, so I do not dare to do anything more emphatic, but I hope that perhaps it will be thought I am a masquerader, for always at these political meetings there are secret police listening. When I heard the instruction from the BBC——"

"Which reminds me." Fen reached for the telephone, dialled a number, asked for a certain extension, spoke, listened, chuckled.

"It seems," he told them, ringing off, "that quite a surprising number of German-speakers listen to 'Music for the Multitude'. They've all been ringing up wanting to know why the BBC should suppose that 'Anchors Aweigh' is based on the German folk-song 'The tall man at the bar will give you a signal: then, German Comrade, please go straight to the Gents.' "

Sir Somebody laughed. But Campbell, the fourth member of the party, said rather irritably: "I still don't see it; I still don't see how you could tell from that meeting, that Herr Dietrich was wanting to stay in this country."

"Oh, simple," said Fen. "He pronounced 'Eisenhower' wrong. Despite the spelling of the last two syllables, it's a German name, of course, which every German recognizes as such. What's more, we in England and America pronounce it exactly as a German would. 'Eisssenhoer', from a Berliner, was just ridiculous. Either Herr Dietrich wasn't Herr Dietrich at all, or else he was relying on the Stepney Communist Party's ignorance of German—as I relied on it in arranging for that broadcast message—to send out a distress signal. Ike to the rescue! A good thing, in the circumstances, that they didn't elect Stevenson."

A COUNTRY TO SELL

"So what it comes down to," said the young American, in a voice which no amount of self-discipline could keep entirely steady, "is just this: either this top guy in Washington is a traitor, or I am. The FBI's picked me for the honour—and if they could get any kind of concrete evidence against me, I'd be going back to the States for a long, long spell in gaol. Even as it is—well, but never mind me. All I'm saying now, in italics, capitals, is that I was NOT careless and I did NOT sell out. And if you accept that, there's only the one alternative."

Gervase Fen, in whose rooms at St Christopher's the conversation was taking place, regarded his visitor thoughtfully. "In strict grammar," he observed, "there is of course never more than one alternative; sometimes, though, the list of candidates for the position is rather larger than one imagines . . ." He hesitated. "Look, Christopher, why have you come to me?"

Christopher Bradbury considered; then he answered slowly: "I guess I just had to tell somebody. A man can't keep a thing like this boiling inside of him indefinitely without going haywire. And the question now is, do you believe I'm telling the truth?"

"Yes, I do," Fen assured him. "But before I say anything more than that, I'd like to go over the facts once again and make sure there's nothing I've missed.

"Like this: On going down after a mis-spent career here at Oxford, you got a job in a top-secret department of the FBI, working in London in collaboration with our Special Branch."

"Check," said Bradbury.

"Your only relative in England is—no, was: you said he'd just died, didn't you?—was a step-brother of your mother's, an elderly retired lawyer called Darling who lived in Sussex by the sea."

"Check."

"Last month you were given a fortnight's leave; and you went to Sussex for the second week of it to stay with Darling. There

you met, among other people, a family called Anderson—
mother, father, grown-up daughter—who were old acquain-
tances of Darling's and who had rented a house near by for their
summer holiday.

"On the day before you left you were due to telephone direct
to your top man in Washington for instructions. Your uncle was
in poor health, and more or less permanently confined to one
room—and unfortunately that was the room with the telephone
in it. So rather than embark on the insane enterprise of trying to
get through to Washington from a public call-box, you went
along to the Andersons' house and asked to use *their* telephone."

"So far, correct."

"The Andersons"—Fen went on—"showed you into the parlour, where the telephone was, and left you alone there. You
closed and fastened the door and the windows, so that even if
anyone had been listening outside them, they could have heard
nothing. And——"

"And also," said Bradbury, "I made sure—it was just routine,
of course, but I was still thorough about it—that there were no
ventilators, to let out sound, and no hidden persons or recording
machines."

"Good. You then picked up the telephone and asked for your
number. I'm not quite clear about these technical precautions
you mentioned . . ."

"If anyone asks for that particular number," Bradbury
explained, "by the time the exchange rings him back he's through
to a special switchboard, on a line which can't be tapped and has
no operators to overhear. The FBI checked that part of
it—naturally—and it was foolproof. That has to be accepted,
whether we like it or not."

"All right. You got through, were given your instructions, rang
off, thanked and paid the Andersons, and went back to your
uncle."

"And twelve hours later, before I'd even left Sussex," Bradbury concluded grimly, "a valuable man was shot dead in Hamp-
stead, and months of work collapsed in ruins, because those
instructions were known.

"Not even my colleagues or my boss in this country, not even
your Special Branch, had any idea what those instructions would
be. It wasn't necessary for me to pass them on, any part of them,

to anybody, and they weren't written down. They went direct into my head, and that's where they stayed."

And with a despairing gesture Bradbury fell back in his chair. "So what, I ask you, is the answer to that?"

Fen chose to regard the question as rhetorical; and a heavy silence descended on the room. Presently, without much appearance of optimism: "I can understand," Fen ventured, "how the line from your special switchboard to Washington could be made safe from tapping. But the line from the Anderson house to the switchboard, now . . ."

Bradbury shook his head. "No soap. They have instruments to detect if a line's being tapped, and this line just wasn't."

"In that case there's got to be something you haven't told me . . . These Andersons, for instance. What sort of people are they?"

"Ordinary. Middle class. Fairly well off, I'd say. Not intellectual giants, but reasonably lively and pleasant. Marion, that's the daughter, was crazy about some guy her parents didn't approve of—he wasn't down there in Sussex, though . . ." Bradbury paused. "Yes, go on," said Fen impatiently.

"About Marion? Well, naturally she was wanting to marry this guy. She knew her parents thought he was after her for her money—she has a bit of her own—so that was holding her back. But I got the idea that if they'd seriously tried to prevent her seeing him, she'd have eloped with him there and then: she's twenty-five, twenty-six maybe, so there'd have been nothing to stop her. Mind you, she didn't seem too happy about things . . ."

Bradbury's voice trailed away; then with more energy he said: "Look, Gervase, I don't see how all this stuff about Marion——"

"Stop grumbling," said Fen peevishly. "What I was wondering, you see, was whether . . ." And at that he too broke off, so that again the silence stretched between them. Bradbury noted, however, that his ex-tutor's lean and ruddy countenance no longer wore its look of distressing blankness; it was alert now, and grew more so momently as Bradbury watched . . .

"Christopher," said Fen abruptly. "Do you want my advice?"

"What would that be?"

"My advice," said Fen, "is that you go to Mr Anderson and ask him to tell you, in confidence, if there wasn't something a bit odd about that telephone in the house he rented."

Bradbury stared. *"Odd?"* he echoed. "There was no exten-sion, if that's what you mean——"

"No, no."

"And if by any chance you're thinking that the instrument itself can have had some sort of a dictaphone hidden inside it, I can assure you, most earnestly——"

"Don't *argue*, Christopher," Fen interrupted him. "Just go away and do as I say."

So Bradbury looked at him again; and thereupon ceased to argue, and went away and did as he said.

And certainly it was a transfigured American who returned to Fen's rooms the following evening.

"Sherlock does it again!" he crowed inanely. "The deductions of the great man proved beyond question that——"

"Not deductions," said Fen with some rancour. "Intelligent guess-work—nothing more." He is fond of compliments, but likes accuracy even better. "Have a drink and tell me about it."

"Well, here's how it must have happened," said Bradbury as soon as he was supplied. "Our—our opponents, let's call them, get hold of my uncle and suggest that information he can give them about my activities will be well paid for. Since I myself have been keeping that possibility firmly in mind, he isn't too hopeful.

"But then his friends the Andersons come down to the neigh-bourhood to stay. Pa and Ma are on hot bricks because daughter Marion has fallen for a jerk. They daren't thwart her openly; but they know said jerk has promised to telephone Marion every evening while she's away.

"So when clever old Mr Darling suggests that they put a wrong telephone number—*his* number—on to the instrument in the house they've rented, they think that's just fine: Marion will give the transferred number to the boy-friend; the boy-friend will phone Mr Darling—thinking it's the Anderson house; and Mr Darling, representing himself as a friend of the family who's on Marion's side, will tell him that Marion's ill, but will get in touch with him later, and also that he's not to write, because with Marion confined to bed there's a chance his letters will be inter-cepted and withheld.

"The boy-friend will believe all this: 'Marion's nuts about me,' he'll tell himself: 'if she *weren't* ill, she'd certainly be hanging around the phone waiting for me to call—so this literally *can't* be just a trick to choke me off.' But meanwhile, of course, Marion will be wondering why the heck she's not hearing from him—and she can't write him or phone him herself, because he's a commercial traveller moving around the country all the time, and she doesn't know where he'll be. So maybe, with any luck, she'll decide he's neglecting her badly, and react accordingly. Even if she does subsequently meet him again, his explanations, when you come to think of it, are going to sound very, very fishy indeed . . .

"But of course, it isn't Marion's welfare that clever old Mr Darling has chiefly in mind: what interests him about the set-up is the possibility of tripping *me*—because so long as I have any private long-distance calls to make, the Anderson house is the likeliest place for me to go.

"And I fall for it. So help me, the one thing no one *ever* questions is the number set into the dial of a phone. Naturally I gave it to the exchange when they had to call me back; so that when the connection was made, the house they actually called was my uncle's. He imitated my voice—he'd been expecting something——"

"No password?" Fen interposed rather brusquely.

"What? Password? Hell, no. The Washington number I called was password enough in itself: any unauthorized person capable of worming *that* number out of me would be quite capable of worming out a couple dozen passwords as well . . .

"Where was I? Yeah, well, the rest's obvious, I guess. My uncle imitates me in talking to the boss in Washington; then he rings the real number of the Anderson house and imitates the boss in talking to me. Circle complete."

"H'm," said Fen. "Your uncle was taking a good fat risk, though."

"Old buzzard!" And Bradbury scowled ferociously. "But no, there couldn't be any serious risk. Not for him. He was dying, you see, and knew it. The only thing was, he'd run through all his money . . .

"And clever old Mr Darling wasn't going to any pauper's grave so long as he had a nephew, and a man's life, and a country to sell."

A CASE IN CAMERA

DETECTIVE INSPECTOR HUMBLEBY, of New Scotland Yard, had been induced by his wife to spend the first week of his summer's leave with his wife's sister, and his wife's sister's husband, in Munsingham, and was correspondingly aggrieved.

Munsingham, large and sooty, seemed to him not at all the place for recreation and jollity; moreover, his wife's sister's husband, by name Pollitt, was, like himself, a policeman, being superintendent of the Munsingham City CID, so that inevitably shop would be talked.

On the second day of the visit, however, Humbleby's grievances were erased from his mind by the revelation of a serious crisis in his brother-in-law's affairs.

"I'm going to be retired," said Pollitt abruptly that evening, over tankards in the pub. "I haven't got round to telling Marion about it yet."

Humbleby was staring at him in amazement. "Retired? But you're not nearly at retirement age yet. Why on earth——"

"Because I've got across the chief constable," said Pollitt. "He wanted a case to be considered closed—with perfectly good reason, I must say—and I wanted it kept open. I did keep it open, too, for a week or so—against his orders. Several of my men were tied up with it when they ought to have been doing other things.

"I didn't have the least excuse. I was going on instinct, and the fact that a couple of witnesses were just a bit too consistent in their stories to be true . . . If I *did* possess definite evidence that the facts in this case aren't what they seem, I could put it up to the Watch Committee, and I'm pretty sure they'd uphold me. In fact, it wouldn't come to that; the CC'd withdraw. But definite evidence is just what's lacking—so . . ." And Pollitt shrugged resignedly.

"M'm," said Humbleby. "Just what is this case?"

"Well, if you don't mind coming along to my office tomorrow morning, and having a look at the dossier . . ."

*   *   *

And the basic facts of the case, Humbleby found, were in themselves simple enough.

A month previously, on 27 June, between 10.30 and 11.00 in the morning (the evidence as to these times being positive and irrefragable), a fifty-year-old woman, a Mrs Whittington, had been murdered in the kitchen of her home on the outskirts of the town.

The weapon—a heavy iron poker, with which Mrs Whittington had been struck violently on the back of the head—was found, wiped clean of fingerprints, near by. The back door was open, and it was evident that the murder had followed, or been followed by, a certain amount of pilfering.

Mrs Whittington's husband, Leslie Whittington, a man younger and a good deal better-looking than his wife, held the post of chief engineer in the machine-tool manufacturing firm of Heathers and Bardgett, whose factory was some ten minutes' walk from the Whittington home.

On the morning in question Whittington had been, as usual on weekdays, in his office at the factory. And the only respect in which, from his point of view, this particular morning had differed from any other was that he had been visited by a reporter, a girl, who worked for the most important of the Munsingham local newspapers. This girl, by name Sheila Pratt, was doing a series on the managers and technicians of Munsingham industry, and Whittington, an important man in his line, represented her current assignment.

She had arrived at Whittington's office shortly before 10.30 and had left again three-quarters of an hour later. During this period Whittington's secretary had, on Whittington's own instructions, told callers, and people who telephoned, that Whittington was out, thereby ensuring that the interview remained undisturbed.

Moreover, there was a fire-escape running down past Whittington's office window to a little-frequented yard.

As a matter of course, Pollitt had set in train the routine of investigating whether some previous association could have existed between Whittington and Sheila Pratt. Their own assertion was that until the interview they had been complete strangers to one another; but Mrs Whittington, Pollitt had learned, was not the divorcing sort—and the pilfering could easily have been a blind.

Before any results could be obtained from this investigation, however, there had occurred that development which had resulted in the chief constable's ordering the file on the case to be closed. Two days after the murder, a notorious young thug called Miller was run over and killed by a lorry on the by-pass road, and in his pocket were found several small pieces of jewellery looted from Mrs Whittington's bedroom at the time of her death.

"There were witnesses, too," said Pollitt, "who'd seen Miller hanging about near the Whittington house on the morning Mrs W was done in. So it was reasonable enough to put the blame on him, and just leave it at that. Of course, Miller could quite well have come along and pinched the stuff *after* the murder was committed, but the CC thought that in the absence of any evidence against the husband that was stretching it a bit far, and one sees his point of view."

"One does," Humbleby agreed. "And I must admit, Charlie, that at the moment I still don't quite see yours."

"I know, I know," said Pollitt, disgruntled. "But I still maintain that those two—Whittington and the Pratt girl—had their story far too pat. I took them both through it several times—separately, and with all sorts of camouflage stuff about unimportant detail—and neither of them ever put a foot wrong. Look." He thrust a sheaf of typescript at Humbleby. "Here are their various statements. *You* have a look at them."

"M'm," said Humbleby, nearly an hour later. "Yes . . . Look, Charlie, the girl's statements all contain stuff about the camera she brought with her to the interview. 'Tripod . . . three seconds' exposure'—all that. Do you happen to have copies of the pictures she took?"

"She only kept one," said Pollitt. "But I've got a blow-up print of that, all right." He produced it and handed it across. "It's a good picture, isn't it?"

It was unusually sharp and clear, showing Whittington at his desk with the desk clock very properly registering ten minutes to eleven.

"But there's nothing in it that's any help, that I can see," Pollitt went on. "The clothes are right. The——"

"Just a minute," Humbleby interrupted sharply. He had

reverted from the photograph to the signed statements of Sheila Pratt, and was frowning in perplexity. "It's possible that—I say, Charlie, is this girl an experienced photographer—a professional, I mean?"

Pollitt shook his head. "No, she's just a beginner. I understand she's only bought her camera quite recently. But why——"

"And this factory," said Humbleby. "Is there a lot of heavy machinery? A lot of noise and vibration?"

"Yes, there is. What are you getting at?"

"A couple more questions and you'll see it for yourself. Is Whittington's office somewhere *over* the factory? Can you feel the vibration *there*?"

"You can. But I still don't understand——"

"You will, Charlie. Because here's the really critical query. *Were those machines running continuously during the whole of the time Sheila Pratt was in Whittington's office?*"

And with that, Pollitt realized. "Tripod," he muttered. Then his voice rose. "Time-exposure . . . Wait." He grabbed the telephone, asked for a number, asked for a name, put his question, listened, thanked his informant, and rang off. "Yes, they were running," he said triumphantly. "They were running all right."

And Humbleby chuckled. He flicked the photograph with his forefinger. "So that very obviously this beautifully clear picture wasn't taken at the time when Sheila Pratt and Whittington allege it was taken—because tripod plus time-exposure plus vibration would inevitably have resulted in blurring . . . I imagine they must have faked it up one evening, after the factory had stopped work; and the girl was too inexperienced in photography to realize the difference that that would make in the finished product . . .

"Well, Charlie, will your chief like it, do you think?"

Pollitt grinned. "He won't like it at all. But give the devil his due, he'll swallow it all right." He hesitated. "So that solves my own personal problem—and I needn't tell you how grateful I am . . . But as to whether we can get a prosecution out of it——"

They never did. "And really, it was a good thing," said Pollitt two years later in London, when he and his wife were returning the Humblebys' visit, and the conversation had turned to the topic of Whittington and his fate. "Because if the DPP had allowed it to be taken to court, the chances are he'd have been acquitted in spite of the lies and in spite of the information we dug out about the surreptitious meetings between him and the Pratt girl in the eighteen months before the murder.

"And if he *had* been acquitted—well, he wouldn't have needed to worry about the possibility of his new wife giving him away, would he? And he wouldn't have set about stopping her mouth in that clumsy, panicky fashion . . .

"And they wouldn't be hanging him for it at Pentonville at nine o'clock tomorrow morning . . . What a bit of luck, eh?"

BLOOD SPORT

"I'VE HEARD FROM the ballistics people," said Superintendent MacCutcheon, "and they tell me there's no doubt whatever that the bullet was fired from Ellingham's gun. Is that what you yourself were expecting?"

"Oh, yes." At the other side of the desk, in the first-floor office at New Scotland Yard, Detective Inspector Humbleby nodded soberly. "Yes, I was expecting that all right," he said. "Taken together with the rest of the evidence, it makes a pretty good case."

"And your own report?"

Humbleby handed over a sheaf of typescript. "No verdict?" queried MacCutcheon, who had turned immediately to the final page.

"Certainly there's a verdict." Humbleby paused. "Implicit, I mean," he added. "You'll see."

"Nice of you," said MacCutcheon. "Nice of you DI's to try and keep my tottering intellect alive with little games. Well, I'll buy it. Smoke if you care to." And he settled down to read, while Humbleby, leaning back in his chair and lighting a cheroot, reconsidered the salient features of his visit to Harringford the previous day . . .

He had arrived there by train, with Detective Sergeant Pinder in tow, shortly before midday; and they had gone at once to the police station. Inspector Bentinck, who received them, proved to be a bony, discontented-looking man of fifty or thereabouts.

"Between ourselves," he said, as he led them to his office, "our County CID are a fairly feeble lot at the moment, so I'm glad the CC had the sense to call you people in straight away. And of course, having a ruddy lord involved . . . You knew that, did you?"

"It's about the only thing I do know," said Humbleby.

"I've got his gun here." They had reached the office, and Bentinck was unlocking a cupboard, from which presently he produced a .360 sporting rifle. Two slats of wood were tied to either side of the breech, and there was a loop of string for carrying the weapon.

"Not been tested for prints yet," said Humbleby intelligently; and Bentinck shook his head.

"Not been touched since I confiscated it yesterday morning. But in any case I shouldn't think you'll get any prints off it except his—Lord Ellingham's, I mean. He'd cleaned it, you see, by the time I caught up with him."

"Well, well, we can try," said Humbleby. "Pinder's brought all his paraphernalia with him. See what you can get, please," he added to the sergeant. "And meanwhile"—to Bentinck—"let's have the whole story from the beginning."

So Pinder went away to insufflate and photograph the rifle, and Bentinck talked. "Ellingham's one of what they call the backwoods peers," he said. "He's got a big estate about five miles from here, but I shouldn't think there's much left in the family coffers, because he lives in the lodge, not in the manor-house—that's shut up. He's about fifty, not married, lives alone.

"Well now, like everyone else, Ellingham's had his servant problems, and just recently—for the last year or so, that is—the only person he's been able to get to look after him has been this girl."

"Enid Bragg."

Bentinck assented. "Enid Bragg. And a fortnight ago even she packed it in—since when Ellingham's had to look after himself."

"What sort of girl was she?"

"Not bad looking in a trashy sort of way," said Bentinck. "I don't know that there's much else good to say about her . . . Anyway, point is, this Enid lives—lived—in a cottage with her parents not far from the Ellingham estate. And it was yesterday morning, while she was waiting for the 8.50 bus so as to come into town and do a bit of shopping, that someone picked her off with a rifle, presumably from behind the hedge opposite the bus-stop.

"Well, of course, when the bus came along, there she was with a hole in her head, and it wasn't long before me and the sergeant got out there and took over. We went through all the usual motions, but the only worthwhile thing we got out of it was the bullet." Bentinck opened a drawer in his desk and produced a small jeweller's box in which a squashed rifle bullet lay on a bed

of cotton wool. "It'd gone clean through her and buried in an ash tree behind the bus-stop."

"No cartridge-case?"

"Not that we've been able to find. So I said to myself, well, better look up Ellingham first, because I knew he'd got a gun, and after all, the girl had been working for him until just recently, and what should I find but that——"

Here Bentinck broke off at the return of Pinder, who announced that he had dusted and photographed the two or three blurred prints on the rifle, and that it was now at everyone's disposal. Taking it from him, Humbleby squinted down the barrel.

"Clean as a new pin," he said cheerfully. But Pinder noticed that something had made him more than usually pensive.

"Well, that's it, you see," continued Bentinck, not very lucidly. "When I got to the lodge, there was Ellingham cleaning that thing, and it turned out he'd been out on his own, looking for something to shoot, since eight o'clock. I took the gun away from him, with all the usual gab about routine, and I'll say this for him, he didn't make any fuss about it. And until we see whether the murder bullet came from it, that's really all—oh, except for the autopsy. Five months gone, our Enid was."

"Oh, Lord," said Humbleby in genuine dismay. "Not that again. The number of times——"

"Yes, it's common enough, I suppose. Ah, well. If you get a nasty sort of girl like Enid Bragg into trouble, you must expect a bit of blackmail. And the only certain way of putting a stop to it——"

"Damn!" Thus Superintendent MacCutcheon, breaking in violently on Humbleby's thoughts in the first-floor office at Scotland Yard. He had finished reading the report, and now whacked it down angrily on the desk in front of him.

There was a long silence.

"Not pleasant," said MacCutcheon at last.

"Not pleasant at all, sir," Humbleby agreed. From the particular expression on his superior's face he was in no doubt that the evidence had been interpreted correctly. "And I don't think we're going to be able to pin the murder on him, either. There's no alibi—that much I found out before I left. And if we worked hard at it, I dare say we could establish the connection with the girl. But we'll never find the bullet, and without that——"

"We shall have to try," said MacCutcheon grimly. "If it's just a charge of fabricating evidence people will think he only did it to get a conviction. That's damaging enough, of course, but even so . . ."

He reached for a blue-bound book from the shelves behind him, and riffled through the pages until he found what he wanted.

"Gross's *Criminal Investigation*," he announced. "Third edition page 157. 'A rifle barrel reasonably clean on one day will show plain traces of fouling next day. In such cases the barrel sweats after it has been cleaned.'

"But when you looked at it, the barrel of Ellingham's rifle was perfectly clean."

"Yes."

"It oughtn't to have been, if Bentinck's story was true."

"No."

"So Bentinck, the only person with access to that rifle, had recently cleaned it."

"Yes."

"And there'd be no point in his cleaning it unless he'd fired it."

"No."

"And there'd be no point in his firing it, and subsequently lying, unless he happened to want a bullet to substitute for the real murder bullet which he dug out of the tree."

Again there was silence. "I suppose there's no chance we're wrong?" MacCutcheon burst out fretfully. "I mean, there were even traces of blood and brains on that bullet he gave you . . . I suppose——"

"No, no chance at all." Humbleby was definite. "As to the traces—Well, after all, a quick visit to the mortuary with a—a pair of tweezers, say . . . "

"Yes." MacCutcheon relapsed into gloom again. "Yes . . . What gun do you think he used to kill the girl?"

"His own, I imagine. I got a look at the register, and he certainly has one, and it's a .360 all right. But his sergeant told me he'd hardly ever used it—which would account for his not realizing about the fouling." Humbleby rose. "He had one morning's shooting, it seems, years ago, and after that never went out again . . . No stomach for blood sports, the sergeant said."

THE PENCIL

IT WAS NOT until the third night that they came for Eliot.

He had expected them sooner, and in his cold, withdrawn fashion had resented and grown impatient at the delay—for although his tastes had never been luxurious, the squalid bedroom which he had rented in the Clerkenwell boarding-house irked him.

Now, listening impassively to the creak of their furtive steps on the staircase, he glanced at his gun-metal wrist-watch and made a certain necessary adjustment in the hidden thing that he carried on him. Then quite deliberately he turned his chair so that his back was towards the door.

His belated dive for his revolver, after they had crept up behind him, was convincing enough to draw a gasp from one of them before they pinioned his arms, thrusting a gun-muzzle inexpertly at the back of his neck.

Petty crooks, thought Eliot contemptuously, as he feigned a struggle. And, "petty crooks," again, as they searched him and hustled him down to the waiting car.

Yet his scorn was not vainglorious. The hard knot into which his career of professional killing had twisted his emotions left no room even for that. Only once had Eliot killed on his own account—and that was when they had nearly caught him. He was not proposing to repeat the mistake.

It was a little after midnight, and the narrow street was deserted. The big car moved off smoothly and quietly. Presently it stopped by an overgrown bomb site, blanched under the moon, and the blinds were drawn down. There they gagged Eliot, and blindfolded him, and tied his hands behind his back. When they found him submissive, their confidence perceptibly grew.

Between them and Addison's lot, Eliot reflected as the car moved off again, there was little or nothing to choose: petty crooks, all of them, petty warehouse thieves whose spheres of operation had happened to collide. That was why he was here.

He made no attempt to chart mentally the car's progress. He

had not been asked to do that—and it was Eliot's great merit as a hireling murderer that he was incurious, never going beyond the letter of his commission. Leaning back against the cushions, he reconsidered his instructions as the car purred on through London, through the night.

"Holden's people are getting to be a nuisance," Addison had said—Addison the young boss with his swank and his oiled hair and his Hollywood mannerisms. "But if Holden dies, they'll fall to pieces. That's your job—to kill Holden."

Eliot had only nodded. Explanations bored him.

"But the trouble is," Addison had continued, "that we can't find Holden. We don't know where his hide-out is. That means we've got to fix things so that they lead us to it themselves. My idea is to make you the bait." He had grinned. "Poisoned bait."

With that he had gone on to explain how Eliot was to be represented as a new and shaky recruit to the Addison mob; how it was to be made to seem that Eliot possessed information which Holden would do much to get.

Eliot had listened to what concerned him directly and ignored the rest. It was thorough, certainly. They ought to fall for it.

And, to judge from his present situation, they had.

It seemed a long drive. The one thing above all others that Holden's men wanted to avoid was the possibility of being followed, the possibility that he, Eliot, might pick up some clue to the hide-out's whereabouts. So whatever route they were taking, it certainly wasn't the most direct.

At last they arrived. Eliot was pushed upstairs and through a door, was thrust roughly on to a bed. A bed, he thought: good. That meant that Holden had only this one musty-smelling room. All the more chance, therefore, that the job would come off.

He let them hit him a few times before he talked: his boyhood had inured him to physical pain, and he was being well paid. Then he told them what they wanted to know—the story Addison had given him, the story with just enough truth in it to be convincing. Eliot enjoyed the acting: he was good at it. And they were at a disadvantage, of course, in that having left the blindfold on they were unable to watch his eyes.

In any case, Holden—who to judge from his voice was a nervous, elderly Cockney—seemed satisfied. And Holden was the only one of them who mattered.

Before long, Eliot knew, the police would get Holden, and Addison, too, and their small-time wrangling for the best cribs would be done with for good and all.

That, however, was of no consequence to Eliot. All he had to do was to say his lesson nicely and leave his visiting card and collect his fee. And here it was at last: the expected, the inevitable offer. Yes, all right, Eliot said smoothly after a few moments' apparent hesitation; he didn't mind being their stool-pigeon so long as they paid him enough. And they were swallowing that, too, telling him what they wanted him to find out about Addison's plans, sticking a cigarette between his bruised lips and lighting it for him.

He almost laughed. They weren't taking off the blindfold, though; they didn't trust him enough for that. They were going to let him go, but in case he decided not to play ball with them after all, they weren't risking his carrying away any important news about them.

They were going to let him go. This is it, Eliot thought. And delicately, as he lay sprawled on the bed, his fingers moved under the hem of his jacket, so that, hidden from his interrogators, something slim and smooth rolled out on to the bedclothes.

Fractionally he shifted his position, thrusting the object, to the limit that the rope round his wrists would allow, underneath the pillow. It was a nice little thing, and Eliot was sorry to lose it: in appearance, nothing more than an ordinary propelling pencil, but with a time-fuse inside it and a powerful explosive charge.

Addison had told him that it was one of the many innocent-looking objects supplied to French saboteurs during the Occupation, to be deposited on the desks of German military commanders or in other such strategic places. Eliot had appreciated its potentialities. As a means of murder it was chancy, of course: this one might kill Holden, or on the other hand it might kill a maidservant making up the bed.

But that was none of Eliot's business. He was doing what he had been told to do, and whether it succeeded or not, he was going to collect.

The return drive was a replica of the first. At the bomb-site the gag and bonds and blindfold were taken off, and presently Eliot was back at his lodging-house door, in the grey light of early dawn, watching Holden's car drive rapidly away.

He mounted to his room, examined his damaged face without resentment in the mirror, on an impulse started to pack. Then, tiring suddenly, he lay down on the bed and slept. The pencil had been set to explode at eight.

It was a quarter to eight when Eliot woke, and the full light had come. Finish packing first, he thought, then see Addison and report. The early editions of the evening papers would tell him before he caught the boat-train whether Holden was dead or not.

So he was shifting the pillows, to make more room on the bed for his big, shabby suitcase, just as the clock of St John's struck the hour.

And that was when he saw the pencil.

For a second he stared at it in simple incomprehension. Then understanding came. Of course, thought Eliot dully, of course. They weren't risking the secret of their precious hide-out. This is where they brought me to, after driving me round and round the streets. This is where they questioned me—here in my own room.

Panic flooded him. He ran. From the bedside to the door was a distance of no more then three paces.

But the explosion had caught and killed him before his fingers even touched the knob.

WINDHOVER COTTAGE

"Mrs Cowen?"

"Yeah, I'm Mrs Cowen."

"Detective Sergeant Robartes, madam. Scotland Yard. If I could just have a brief word with you——"

"Well!" Wendy Cowen's laugh was a fraction unsteady. "Has your Immigration Department changed its mind and decided I'm an undesirable alien or something?"

"Nothing like that, Mrs Cowen. It's about your husband, Dr Philip Cowen."

"Phil!" Wendy stared. "Not—not an accident?"

"No, your husband's quite well, madam. It's just that there's been a—a little bit of trouble at this cottage he rented near Awton, and the Yard asked me to find you and take you down there. If we catch the 10.18 train——"

"Trouble?" Wendy exclaimed. "Look, Sergeant, try to be a little more specific, will you, please?"

"Well, Mrs Cowen, it seems that when your husband got back to the cottage last evening from his usual walk, he—well, to be blunt about it, he found a girl dead in the parlour. Of course, he reported the discovery to the police, straight away. And of course, they're having to look into it. Incidentally, Mrs Cowen, we understood from your husband that you weren't due in England till this evening."

"I managed to get away 24 hours earlier than I'd expected. Pan-American notified me of a last-minute cancellation on yesterday's flight, so I switched my booking to that."

"Ah. A good thing we took the trouble to check their passenger lists, then. You spent last night here in your husband's flat, I take it?"

"Sure. I didn't have a key, but I showed my identification to the janitor and he let me in."

"Yes, we guessed you'd probably have come here. Dr Cowen was worried, you see, about not being able to get up to London to meet you when you arrived."

Wendy Cowen gestured impatiently. "Let's cut out the small talk, Sergeant, shall we? Whatever it is, tell me. I can take it."

Robartes eyed her thoughtfully; and decided that probably she could. He said: "This girl was murdered, you see." And she nodded slowly, biting her lip.

"Yeah. That was indicated. And you think—you think Phil did it?"

"I said nothing about that."

"Okay, okay," she answered wearily. "Skip it. How far is this place, this cottage? Could we drive there?"

"Certainly, if you'd rather."

"I have a Jaguar, you see, a brand-new one. It was going to be a surprise for Phil. . . . Mail-order, sort of. They had it waiting for me at the airport when I stepped off the plane—I'd cabled them from New York I was going to be a day earlier, and——"

"But you didn't cable your husband?"

"No, Sergeant, I didn't cable my husband. It was going to be a surprise for him, see? Maybe it still will, at that. . . . Let's get moving, shall we?"

The roads out of London were relatively clear that morning. So was the A30—with the result that by the sergeant's watch it was scarcely more than two hours before they reached Awton, where they stopped to ask for directions. Up till then, they had spoken little. But as, leaving the main road, they drove on beyond the little town, the sergeant fished a pencil and notebook from his pocket, saying:

"There are just one or two things I'd like to check, Mrs Cowen, if you don't mind."

The girl's face was expressionless, mask-like. "Go ahead," she told him.

"You reached the flat about seven last evening?"

"Correct."

"And then?"

"Then? Then I fixed myself a snack out of a can and went to bed. I was tired." She paused, then added: "To start with, I'd had the idea of not stopping off in London at all. I thought I'd drive straight down here from the airport. But by the time we landed I wasn't feeling so good. Airplanes don't agree with me. I guess. Anyway, we weren't planning to keep on the cottage after today.

so I thought I'd stay the night in Town and then drive down this morning and fetch Phil back to the flat."

"Your husband is a research physician?"

"Yeah."

"When did you first meet him?"

"Three, four months ago. He was over in the States, working at Johns Hopkins."

"And it was in the States that you were married?"

"Yeah. We had a two weeks' honeymoon, and then he had to get back here to England. I couldn't come with him because I was working then for a fashion magazine, and couldn't throw up the job in a hurry. So we arranged he should rent some place quiet in the country where he could go ahead and work his material up into a book, and I'd join him as soon as I could get away."

"I see." And there was a silence. Presently Wendy said ironically:

"I wouldn't want you to talk yourself dry, Sergeant, but would it be in order for me to ask just *how* this—this female was killed?"

"She was hit with a poker," said Robartes shortly.

"Uh-huh. And did Phil—I mean, was she someone he *knew*?"

"Yes."

He glanced quickly at her as he said it, but she kept her eyes fixed steadily on the level stretch of road ahead. "A fine thing," she murmured. "A fine thing. . . . " She changed gear, not gently. "And there was I, imagining——"

"We turn right here," Robartes interrupted her. She braked hurriedly, and with no more than inches to spare they scraped into a side turning which the trees had hidden, and began to climb a steep, unexpected hill. ". . . And there was I," Wendy resumed bitterly, "imagining he was the sort of guy that can be faithful for six weeks or so. Well, so I was wrong. . . .

"But Phil Cowen never *killed* anyone, Sergeant, you can take it from me. He just isn't the type."

And so in silence they came to Windhover Cottage; to a garden where a lean, yellow-haired, sullen-looking man was talking with two others, uniformed. At the sound of the car he looked round resentfully. Then he saw who was driving it.

"Wendy!" he ejaculated, hurrying towards her, "What—how did you——"

And then his steps faltered, and he stopped; and a slow flush spread over his face. And Wendy tried a smile.

"Hello, Phil," she said shakily. "Fine reunion you fixed up."

After half an hour's pacing in the garden, Robartes and the local inspector, whose name was Beadnell, had found themselves pleasantly in agreement.

"The girl, Joan Moss, lived with her parents in Awton," Beadnell had told Robartes. "But they didn't have much control over her, and she used to drive out here most evenings to see Cowen, and sometimes to stay the night.

"Yesterday evening she was here with him as usual. And his story is that about nine o'clock he went out for a walk, leaving her at the cottage, and that when he got back at half-past ten, there she was with her head battered in. As simple as that. As to the poker, there are no prints on it except his, none at all—though I'll admit his are a bit blurred. Someone wearing gloves *could* have handled it subsequently."

"Did he meet anyone when he was out walking?" Robartes asked.

"Nobody, it seems. If he ever went out walking at all."

"M'm," said Robartes. "Well, look, Beadnell, here's how I see it. . . " And he went on to explain in detail how he saw it and why.

So then they went into the house, to where Wendy and Philip Cowen waited, and Beadnell said:

"Mrs Cowen, I must ask you to come to the police station for further questioning. Also, it is my duty to warn you that you needn't make any statement if you don't wish to."

"*Me*?" She stared at him. "Look, you surely can't imagine . . . "

"Better not say too much now, Mrs Cowen," Robartes interrupted her. "For your information, our case is that you drove down here last evening, found Joan Moss alone in the cottage (your husband being out walking), interpreted her presence here correctly, killed her in a fit of jealous rage, and then drove back again to London. Your claim to have spent the night in the flat, from seven onwards——"

"Prove it," said Wendy Cowen harshly. "Just *prove* that I was here. If you can."

"And you didn't mind your husband taking the rap, did you?"

said Robartes remorselessly. "For the very good reason that it wasn't love for him that made you kill: it was wounded pride.

"As to proof, I had that staring me in the face all the way down here: though I'll admit I didn't notice it until you made the mistake of changing gear, on a level stretch of road, just before we came to a hidden turning which led up an unexpected steep hill. A driver doesn't do that sort of thing unless he's been in the neighbourhood before."

"You're crazy!" she exclaimed. "Even if I did do that—and there's only your word for it——"

"Oh, quite, Mrs Cowen," said Robartes smoothly. "I wouldn't say it was *conclusive*, at all. Still, your car was new only yesterday, wasn't it? So I think that while you're having your little chat with Beadnell, we'll get a mechanic along to make sure the mileage indicator is working properly.

"And really, you know, I expect he'll find that it is."

THE HOUSE BY THE RIVER

No, THE HOUSEKEEPER said, she was sorry, but the chief constable still wasn't back from London. He ought to be arriving any time now, though, so if the superintendent would care to wait. . . . The superintendent said that he would wait in the garden.

But it was the farmhouse across the river, rather than the gentle airs of the October evening, which made him decide to stay out of doors.

At first he was resolute in ignoring its obsessive summons. Then, as time wore on, his determination weakened. And presently (as in his heart of hearts he had known must happen in the end); he found himself crossing the leaf-strewn front lawn, found himself halted by the bedraggled hedge at the far side and staring over the stream at the outhouse where Elsie the servant-girl had kept her last assignation. . . .

Death by strangling.

Across the river, a figure, unidentifiable in the failing light, was emerging from the stables, was trudging through the yard. It was Gregson, obviously: Gregson the retired Indian Civil Servant, Gregson the tenant of the farmhouse, Gregson the widower, Gregson the pathetic, Gregson the bore: Gregson who had no doubt been fussing in the stables over the horse he had bought that morning. . . . Glumly the superintendent watched him until he disappeared from view. In a few weeks' time the superintendent, too, would be retiring.

And: I'll be glad to be done with it, he said to himself now: my God, yes, I'll be glad to get away from it all.

The sound of a car roused him, and he returned to the house. "Here we are, sir," he said with a cheerfulness he was far from feeling, as he helped the chief constable out of the driving-seat. "Conference go off all right?"

"Hello, Tom." The chief constable was thin and old, and his complexion looked bleached. "The conference? Oh, the usual thing, you know: too many speeches and too few resolutions. Ruddy awful hotel, too."

"What time did you leave Town?"

"Two o'clock."

"Well, that's not bad going. . . . I've had a packet this afternoon, sir. Do you want a bath or a meal or something first, or shall I——"

"No, I'd rather stretch my legs. Let's stroll down to the river."

To start with they walked in silence—the companionable silence of men who have worked together amicably for many years. Then, as they came in sight of the farmhouse on the opposite bank, the superintendent nodded towards it and spoke.

"That's where it happened, sir—almost on your own doorstep, really. It's the servant-girl, Elsie. Throttled in an outhouse some time this afternoon."

The chief constable took his time about assimilating this. Presently he nodded. "Yes, I've only visited Gregson twice," he said. "Mostly it's been the other way about. But I think I remember seeing the girl."

"I dare say she was striking enough." But the superintendent spoke from inference only: it was a stiff and staring thing, a purple-tongued horror, that he had actually seen. "It wasn't a premeditated job, sir, as far as I can make out. Just someone in a sudden passion. And I had it from Dr Hands that the girl came to him a couple of weeks ago for a pregnancy test: result positive. You can see what that points to."

"Yes." The chief constable's head was hunched down between his shoulders as he stared in front of him into the gathering dusk. "A very well-worn track, that one. . . . Has Gregson still got his nephew staying with him?"

"Yes, he's still there." A flabby, fluttering young man, the superintendent had thought, like the furry, overblown kind of moth. "He and Gregson are the prime suspects, obviously. . . . "

For a moment his voice trailed away; then, with something of an effort: "Seeing that they were neighbours of yours, sir, I didn't——"

"My dear chap, they may be neighbours, but they certainly aren't friends. No, you mustn't let that worry you. But of course, I'm interested to know how they stand."

"Well, sir," said the superintendent, perceptibly relieved, "briefly, it's like this. Dr Hands says the thing happened between one and three, approximately. The body was found by Gregson at about five. They'd had an early lunch, which the girl served, and after that neither of the men set eyes on her—so they say. From lunch onwards the nephew was alone in his room, working. About two o'clock Gregson rode over here to look you up, hoping you'd be back——"

"So he's bought himself a horse at last, has he? He's been talking about it for long enough. . . . Yes, sorry, Tom. Go on."

"Well, he didn't find you, of course, so he rode back again and arrived home about a quarter to three. From then on he didn't see the nephew, and the nephew didn't see him."

The chief constable took his time about this, too. It was a trick, the superintendent reflected, which had been increasingly in evidence since his wife's sudden and tragic death two years before. And God knows, living alone in this great barn of a house with no one but an ageing servant for company——

But by the time the superintendent reached this stage in his meditations, the chief constable was functioning again. "And fingerprints?" he asked.

"Only Gregson's and the girl's and the nephew's so far—what you'd expect. But then, if it was an outsider who did it, he wouldn't have needed to leave any prints. All he'd have to do, if the girl was waiting for him in the outhouse, would be to go through an open gate and an open door, and there he'd be. As to footmarks—well, the ground's as hard as brass."

They had reached the river-bank, and were standing beside a tree half of whose roots had been laid bare by the water's steady erosion. Midges hovered above their heads. On the far bank, the dinghy in which Gregson had been accustomed to scull himself across on his visits to the chief constable bumped lazily against its mooring-post, and in the kitchen window of the farmhouse a light went on. . . .

"Not an easy one, no," the chief constable was saying. "You'll be finding out about Elsie's boy-friends, of course, and I suppose that until you've done that you won't be wanting to commit yourself."

He looked up sharply when there was no reply, and saw that the superintendent was staring out over the water with eyes that had gone suddenly blank. "Tom! I was saying that I imagined. . . . "

But it was a long while before he was answered. And when at last the answer came, it was in the voice of a stranger.

"But you're wrong, sir," said the superintendent, dully. "I know who did it, all right."

Fractionally he hesitated; then: "I tell you frankly," he went on with more vigour, "that I haven't got anything that'd stand up in court. It's like the Rogers case, as far as that goes. . . . It's like the Rogers case in more ways than one."

The chief constable nodded. "I remember. . . . "

And their eyes met, and they understood one another.

And presently the chief constable stirred, saying:

"Yes, I'm glad it's over. I don't know that I ever seriously intended to try and bluff it out, but living's a habit you don't break yourself of very easily, and——Well, never mind all that." He was trying hard to speak lightly. "By the bye, Tom, what did I do—leave my driving licence lying on the outhouse floor?"

"You assumed I said R-O-D-E—as in fact I did—when you ought to have assumed I was saying R-O-W-E-D."

The chief constable considered. "Yes. Yes, I see. If I'd really left Town at lunch-time, I shouldn't have known anything about Gregson's precious horse. Well, well, Tom, I'm not at all sure what the drill is in a situation like this, but I should imagine you'd better get into direct touch with the Home Office."

"There's no case against anyone else, sir." The superintendent's voice was carefully expressionless.

"Thanks very much, but no. Now Vera's dead, nobody——"

He grimaced suddenly. "However, I'm much too much of a coward to want to hang about waiting for the due processes of law. So, Tom, if you don't mind. . . . "

A mile and a half beyond the house, the superintendent stopped his car in order to light a cigarette. But he never looked back. And even in Gregson's farmhouse, where they were starting their makeshift evening meal, no one heard the shot, no one marked, across the dark stream, the new anonymous shadow under the willow tree.

AFTER EVENSONG

THEY WERE STANDING at opposite ends of the living-room, studiously ignoring one another. A little too studiously, the inspector reflected, as, with a sergeant in tow for witness, he stepped inside and closed the door behind him: that elaborate disinterest was as revealing as any demonstrativeness could have been.

"Well now, Mrs Soane, Mr Masters," he said cheerfully, "it's about time we had a little talk. That's providing Mrs Soane feels up to it, of course."

Enid Soane shrugged. She was a faded, worried-looking blonde woman in the middle thirties, a former employee of Soane's whom he had married in his retirement. "I don't mind," she said lifelessly. "I shan't get a wink of sleep tonight anyhow."

"A tragic business." The inspector produced his notebook, perched himself on the arm of a chair. "Not at all the sort of crime you look for in a quiet little village like this. Let's see, now . . . Mr Masters, you'd known Mr Soane for how long?"

Oliver Masters, who had been leaning against the mantelpiece, straightened up abruptly: a thin, dark, middle-aged man, with a hooked nose and a jutting jaw. "Six years," he said. "Ever since he retired from business and became nature correspondent on the *Echo*. I'm on the *Echo* too, you know. That was how we met."

"And did he often invite you here to stay?"

"Fairly often. He rather idealized journalists and journalism, and I don't think he ever quite realized what a dull, unimportant cog in the machine I am. However . . ."

"On this occasion, then, you came down just for the week-end. And earlier this evening the three of you went together to Evensong at the village church."

"Correct."

"After which you and Mrs Soane left Mr Soane in the churchyard and took a walk."

"Yes. Soane had been showing us some of the queer inscriptions on the older tombstones. We suggested a walk, as it was such a fine evening, but he said he wasn't up to it—he suffered a good deal from sciatica, you know. He would sit in the churchyard for a bit, he said, and then go home. So we left him there."

"About what time would that have been?"

"Oh . . . I suppose a quarter or twenty past eight."

"M'm. And where did your walk take you?"

"We cut across the fields towards Hod Hill. Over Lumsden Bridge, past the old mill, and then——"

"Yes. Did you happen to meet anyone you knew?"

Masters frowned. "I don't think . . . Wait, though. We did pass the time of day with an old chap on the bridge. A nice old boy in a shooting-jacket—don't know who he was, but he seemed a respectable sort of citizen."

"Ah, the colonel, that'd be." The inspector smiled. "Colonel Rackstraw. Quite a figure in these parts. Why, I remember him from when I was a boy."

Masters stared. "Are you just guessing, or——"

"No, no. It was the colonel all right. Of course, you haven't heard."

"Haven't heard what?"

"That the colonel was attacked this evening in exactly the same way as Mr Soane—the only difference being that the colonel survived it. It was a courting couple that found him, shortly after nine. He'd been knocked unconscious, and he was just coming round. From what he says, it must have happened fairly soon after you two met him down at Lumsden Bridge."

And at that, Oliver Masters was filled with a sudden wild elation which he was hard put to it to conceal. If he had been a wiser man, he would have known this for what it was—an excessive nervous reaction after an excessive nervous strain, like the snap of a released elastic band.

But Masters was not wise; he was only clever. God, that was bright of me, he thought. For in truth, he remembered the respectable Colonel Rackstraw a great deal better than he had pretended: remembered how the colonel had asked them the time, how, even as he spoke, their ears had caught the faint distant jangle of the church clock's chimes. "Ah—half past," the colonel had said confidently, answering his own question.

But it had not been half past: it had been a quarter to. And Masters, striding along with a distracted Enid at his side, straining instinctively, unreasoningly, to put more distance, and ever more distance, between themselves and the thing that had happened in the churchyard after Evensong, until such time as they could collect themselves and consider what was best to do—Masters had seen, in a flash of inspiration, how the old man's mistake could be turned to their advantage. Leave him to himself, and in due course he was liable to discover the error. But creep back surreptitiously, knock him unconscious with a heavy stone—and how would he know how long he had been dead to the world, how would he know that he had misheard the village clock . . . ?

It had worked, apparently.

"And the colonel didn't see who attacked him?" Masters found himself asking.

"No. But I don't doubt it was the same fellow who killed Mr Soane . . . Incidentally, Mr Masters, the colonel has told us that it was just half past eight when you and Mrs Soane met him at Lumsden Bridge. It occurred to us that he might have come across you while you were out on your walk, and in fact he recognized your description at once. He asked you the time, he says, and——"

"That's true. I'd forgotten. And he's right—it was half past eight." Masters pretended to hesitate. "Is that important?"

"Fairly important, yes. You see, just before I came here this evening I managed at long last to establish, from a combination of factors, that it must have been round about half past when Mr Soane was murdered. So if you two were a good ten minutes' walk away . . ."

"I see," said Masters. "Well, Inspector, I won't make a fuss about your having suspected Enid and me, because obviously you're bound to suspect everybody. But at the same time, I won't pretend I'm not glad the colonel's evidence clears us."

"Oh yes, he's quite definite about it," said the inspector with perfect truth. "We can't shake him . . . By the way, I suppose you checked the time on your own watch? It really was half past?"

"Certainly."

"Your watch is reliable, is it?"

"Yes, perfectly reliable."

The inspector got to his feet. "Well, so now we know where we are." He snapped his notebook shut. "I'm arresting the pair of you for Mr Soane's murder. And I have to warn you that anything you say now may be used in evidence at your trial."

Enid Soane cried out incoherently. She was not a very intelligent woman: for all her lover's explanations, she had never really understood how the attack on the colonel was going to help them, and her instinct had been against it. Now, it seemed, she was being proved right . . .

"Don't be silly, Inspector," Masters was saying with an attempt at coolness. "You've admitted yourself that the colonel's evidence lets us out. Unless you're lying about what the colonel said——"

"No, Mr Masters, I'm not lying."

"Then how can you arrest us?"

"I can arrest you because at half past eight this evening—the time is proved—there was a burglary at Mrs Watling's house here in the village. And because very unfortunately the colonel left his heel-print on a flower-bed in the garden. Poor gentleman, he's always been a little eccentric that way. They only let him out of the Institution just the other day, and now he'll have to go back again.

"But although he's eccentric, he does have what the psychiatrists call insight—and the instinct to cover up. So you see, he too wanted an alibi, and you and Mrs Soane were to supply it. If you hadn't acquiesced in his 'mistake', for your own purposes, I don't think I could have touched you. But as it is . . ."

"All right, Inspector," said Masters shakily. "I'll admit I lied. It wasn't half past when we met this—this madman at the bridge, it was a quarter to. But you can see why I lied, can't you? Although I didn't kill Soane, I had enough sense to realize that I was an obvious suspect, so I seized on the old man's testimony—stupidly, I admit—as a means of clearing myself. That's understandable, isn't it? That's——"

"Yes, Mr Masters, quite understandable. The only trouble about it is that you told your lie a bit too soon in the day. You told it before I'd informed you of the time of Mr Soane's death.

"How could you possibly know that your lie would 'clear' you, as you put it, unless you already knew at what time Mr Soane was killed? And how could you know that, unless you killed him, or saw him killed, yourself?"

And to that, Oliver Masters had no answer, either then or afterwards. None.

DEATH BEHIND BARS

From: The Assistant Commissioner, Criminal Investigation Department, Metropolitan Police.

To: HM Secretary for Home Affairs.

New Scotland Yard,
London, SW1
12 May, 1959

Dear Mr Clunes,

Thank you for your letter dated yesterday. Needless to say, the nature of the questions regarding the Wynter case which Opposition Members are proposing to ask in the House of Commons comes as no particular surprise to me. I have in fact dealt somewhat disingenuously with this matter, as you will see; but to suggest that I have avoided arresting Gellian on account of my personal acquaintance with him is absurd. The outline of the case which follows will, I hope, be sufficient to secure a withdrawal of the questions. If this fails, I shall of course be glad to offer the Members concerned a full and free opportunity to question myself, and the officers who have conducted the investigation, in whatever fashion they think fit.

Their suspicions are the more ironical in that Gellian was in fact arrested only yesterday morning, on my personal instructions. Since the Department of Public Prosecutions regards the evidence against him as insufficient, the arrest was made without a warrant; and within a couple of hours Gellian was inevitably once again a free man. My action did, however, succeed in its intended purpose: Gellian and Mrs Wynter had planned to be married yesterday afternoon; as a result of the scene in my office, the marriage will not now take place. You will say, and rightly, that it is no business of the police to discourage people who wish to marry murderers. None the less, when the intending partner is completely unsuspicious, there is, I believe, a good deal to be said on humane grounds for dropping a hint. In fact, the simple ruse we employed succeeded handsomely, thereby confirming the theory we had formed as to the only possible method by which this (superficially) perplexing murder can have been committed.

Gellian's arrest was so contrived that Mrs Wynter should be with him at the time; she was "allowed" to accompany him to Scotland Yard, and on arrival both of them were brought to my office. Also present were Superintendent Colleano (in charge of the case), Detective Inspector Pugh (who made the arrest), and a shorthand writer (PC Clements). Despite Mrs Wynter's urgings, Gellian declined to send for a solicitor; his attitude was fatalistic throughout, and he looked ill.

I need hardly say that if Gellian's arrest had been anything other than a trick, there would have been no question of my confronting him personally. As it was, I was able to use our previous acquaintance as a pretext for the meeting: I told him, quite untruthfully, that I had just returned from leave, and was anxious for old times' sake to hear an account of the circumstances which had resulted in the Deputy AC's ordering his arrest, and to look into the matter in person; and it is the measure of the queer, apathetic state he was in that he apparently swallowed this preposterous fable without turning a hair.

The proceedings opened with Colleano's giving me a summary of the case. From our point of view, this was mere camouflage; but it is necessary to repeat it here for the purpose of clarifying what happened subsequently.

Approximately two years ago, Dr Harold Wynter, a general practitioner working in the Somerset town of Midcastle, was tried for, and convicted of, the manslaughter of a patient through gross negligence. The evidence against him was by no means decisive, but both judge and jury seem to have been influenced by the fact that he was a morphine addict; he was adjudged guilty and sentenced to imprisonment for three years.

At Nottsville Prison—to which Gellian had a year previously been appointed governor—Wynter's first few weeks were spent in the infirmary where he was weaned of his addiction before being transferred to the cells. Very shortly afterwards, however, he began to suffer from attacks of angina pectoris. Accordingly he was excused from all serious exertion; and in addition —since he proved a model prisoner—was allowed a cell to himself, so that he mingled with the other prisoners only on occasions when light exercise was taken in the yard. His wife, Ellen Wynter, wrote regularly to him, and seems to have visited him as often as she could; these visits were, however, restricted in number owing to the fact that for financial reasons she had been obliged to take a job some considerable distance away.

In the ordinary way of things—taking into account remissions for good conduct—Wynter would have been released in October of this year.

On 23 April, he died in his cell.

This was discovered when luncheon was brought to him at noon of that day. In the absence of contra-indications, the death was taken as being due to angina; for although a man suffering from this complaint may, and often does, live on for a great many years, there is no guarantee that any single attack may not finish him. As with all prison deaths, an inquest was held. But there was no post mortem, since none seemed to be called for, and on the 27th Wynter was buried in the prison cemetery, his death being certified as due to his disease.

There the matter might well have rested. Three days later, however, we received here at Scotland Yard an anonymous letter which accused Gellian of having poisoned Wynter with a plant spray containing nicotine; Gellian's motive, the writer added, was infatuation with Wynter's wife.

I myself ordered that this accusation be investigated, and there proved to be sufficient plausibility in it to justify us in exhuming Wynter's body. The stomach was shown to contain a small but sufficiently lethal quantity of nicotine; in consequence of this a full-scale examination of the circumstances was at once put in hand.

The writer of the anonymous letter was traced easily enough. He was a warder at Nottsville named Parker, who conceived himself to have a grudge against the governor, and who purely by chance had come to hear of the irregular association which did in fact exist between Gellian and Mrs Wynter; the nicotine, he said, was a guess, based on the fact that he knew this type of plant spray to be used occasionally in the governor's shrubbery. It was a suspiciously good guess, and Superintendent Colleano devoted plenty of time and energy to investigating whether Parker himself had opportunity or motive for poisoning Wynter. In the event, however, it was ascertained that he had neither. A second possibility was that Wynter's death had some connection with the death of the patient he was alleged to have neglected; but this again proved impossible to substantiate. To cut a long story short, the closest checking and counter-checking failed to establish a motive for Wynter's death in any of the prison staff excepting Gellian.

Gellian's motive, however, was undeniably a strong one: he was in love with Mrs Wynter. (There is no doubt that Wynter was devoted to his wife, to the extent that—in her view—he would never have agreed to divorce her, no matter what she did; and in spite of his illness, he might well have lived on for many years after his release from Nottsville.) As to the manner in which Gellian and Mrs Wynter became acquainted, that, I think, calls for no detailed description here. It is worth noting, however, that Gellian's obsession with the woman was by no means a happy one. The husband was a prisoner in his personal charge, undergoing a relatively savage sentence for a crime of which he may quite possibly have been innocent; he loved his wife; and finally, he was an incurable invalid. To a man with Gellian's record for probity these considerations may well have been horribly distressing; he himself has said that they worried him deeply—and his anxiety was naturally compounded by the fact that from the official point of view his surreptitious connection with Mrs Wynter was an unforgivable offence for which his resignation would certainly be demanded as soon as the truth became known. As you are aware, that resignation was tendered, and accepted, a fortnight ago. Since Gellian is a wealthy man in his own right, his financial position will scarcely be affected; at the same time, for a man with his long and devoted connection with the penal service, the wrench must have been considerable.

Was Gellian's interest in Mrs Wynter sufficiently strong to over-ride all these considerations? Unquestionably it was; and if so, we may not unreasonably assume that it was strong enough to impel him to the act of murder. He had motive, he had means.

Unfortunately, what he seems quite definitely not to have had is opportunity.

The medical evidence as to the time of Wynter's death, and how long he took to die, is regrettably uncertain; but there is a definite consensus of opinion to the effect that the poison cannot have been ingested earlier than breakfast-time—that is to say, 7.30 am on the day of his death. It seems equally certain, however, that the nicotine was not in Wynter's breakfast; two warders (perfectly reputable men) were concerned in the serving of this, and moreover they were, as it happened, accompanied on this occasion by one of HM Inspectors of Prisons, who had been staying in Nottsville overnight; without going into the matter in detail, I can assure you that short of a conspiracy between these three it is absolutely impossible that the poison can have been administered at this time.

But if not at this time, when? On the morning of his death Wynter did not, as it chanced, require fresh materials for the work he performed in his cell; and the result of this was that the next visit paid to him was at lunch-time, when his body was discovered. It is certain that between 7.30 and noon Wynter was alone in his cell in E block, and that during this period he came in contact neither with Gellian nor with anyone else.

These circumstances would seem to point either to suicide or to murder by trickery (for example, Wynter might previously have been given a preparation of nicotine under the guise of medicine, and have consumed it of his own volition some time on the morning of his death). There exists, however, an insuperable objection to either assumption, in that before breakfast on that particular morning a snap search of the cells in E block was carried out. These searches are routine, but they are not the less thorough for that; and because of the recent suicide of Pickering at Tawton Prison, special attention is currently being paid to the possibility of concealed poison.

The upshot, as regards Wynter, you will guess: no pills or powders or capsules or fluids were found in his cell other than the small supply of trinitrate tablets which he was allowed to keep by him for use in case of an angina attack. Of these, at the time of the search, there were three, in a sealed container; and there is a complex of irrefutable evidence to prove that this same container was still there, still sealed and intact, when Wynter's body was discovered (it was, of course, noticed particularly for the reason that at the time, Wynter's death was assumed to be due to an angina attack sufficiently disabling to have prevented his getting at the tablets).

Now, Gellian's last direct encounter with Wynter had taken

place more than a week before the death; and on that occasion (as always) another member of the prison staff was present (this precaution is so invariable in dealing with convicts that if Gellian had at any time departed from it in his dealings with Wynter, the fact must inevitably have become known to us). How, then, can Gellian or anyone else possibly have supplied Wynter with the means? The three warders who conducted the search on the morning of the death might just conceivably have conspired together to make Wynter a present of poison; but in view of their excellent record, this was not a possibility which Colleano felt able to accept so long as another, and likelier, explanation of the circumstances remained open to him.

And such an explanation did in fact exist. Despite the external appearance of what thriller-writers describe as an "impossible murder" or a "locked-room mystery", the ingenious yet simple way in which Wynter had in fact been murdered was easily deduced from the facts I have given above. Unluckily, proving it in court is quite another matter. The DPP has refused to sanction a prosecution, and I cannot blame him; here, I am sorry to have to say, is one murderer who has been altogether too clever for us.

In reconsidering what I have written, I realize that I have left Mrs Wynter unduly in the background; for in returning Gellian's affection (as she admits she did), she too had cause to wish Wynter dead—a motive all the more powerful in that Gellian is a rich man, while Wynter was not. This motive, however, is offset by the fact that, on the face of it, Mrs Wynter had even less chance of conveying the poison to her husband than Gellian did: the prison staff is convinced that Mrs Wynter cannot have transmitted the nicotine to her husband either through the post—which naturally is strictly censored in Nottsville as in all prisons—or in the course of a visit; and even if this conviction were mistaken, there would still remain the problem of how the poison thus supplied could possibly have escaped notice during the search of Wynter's cell on the morning of his death.

I return now to the scene yesterday morning in my office.

Colleano having finished his account of the case, Mrs Wynter, acutely distressed, urged that her husband's death was almost certainly suicide. She was unable to give any coherent idea of how he could have obtained the poison, or secreted it so effectively as to defy expert search; but she propounded the theory that although she had never explicitly mentioned her association with Gellian to Wynter, he might have come to hear of it through prison rumour, emanating, presumably, in the first instance, from the warder Parker; in support of this notion she mentioned the fact—which she knew from Colleano—that Wynter had destroyed all but a single page (this, presumably, having accidentally escaped his attention) of the many letters she had written him. Furthermore——

But at this point there came an interruption, in the form of a short report addressed to me by the head of our forensic laboratory.

Having scanned this myself, I proceeded to read it aloud.

The single page surviving from Mrs Wynter's correspondence with her husband has been mentioned above; and it was with this that the report was concerned. The page was a part of the very last letter which Wynter received from his wife, delivered to him two days before his death; its news and messages were commonplace; but one of Colleano's subordinates who handled it had been struck by something unusual in the texture of the paper, and had therefore passed it on to the laboratory for examination.

The laboratory's report, though technical in its phraseology, was clear and conclusive: the paper on which the letter was written had been impregnated with a nicotine solution identical with the plant spray that Gellian used in his shrubbery.

When Mrs Wynter heard the contents of the report, she seemed to shrivel. I make no apology for stating her reaction in such melodramatic terms, for never in all my experience have I seen anyone display such plain physical evidences of guilt. This was satisfactory. An actual confession, induced by shock, would have been more satisfactory still; the DPP, however, had already advised us that such a confession would be worthless in court so long as it was unsupported by other evidence, so that we were not unduly cast down by its failure to materialize. Since Mrs Wynter remained silent, Gellian presently asked, in a bewildered fashion, for an explanation. With as much as I could manage of the air of one to whom the truth has at last miraculously been made plain, I gave it.

When Wynter's arrest became imminent (I said), he must have arranged with his wife that in the event of his being sent to prison, she should keep him supplied with morphine by the medium of what are known to United States prison authorities as "satch" letters—i.e. letters written on paper which has been previously saturated in the drug required; so long as these arrive regularly, the chewing and swallowing of them will keep even a confirmed addict fairly happy during the period when his normal sources of supply are cut off. This programme Mrs Wynter was evidently scrupulous in carrying out. But then she met Gellian; noted his infatuation for her; noted that he was a rich man; became aware of the existence of the plant spray in his potting-shed; and at once saw not only how her husband could be murdered, but also how in the process the victim could effortlessly be induced to destroy the evidence against his murderer.

Inevitably, her principal intention was that the death should be assumed to be due to the angina; and but for Parker's grudge against Gellian, that is precisely what would have happened. In case this first line of defence failed, however, Mrs Wynter took a further precaution: she used a poison which could be traced to Gellian, arguing that even if he were to be implicated, arrested and convicted, her hold over him was such that she could persuade him at least to make arrangements for keeping her in comfort during the period of his imprisonment; there might even, she thought, be a fair chance of marrying him before the warrant for his arrest was implemented.

There was little more that I needed to say. Gellian could scarcely have avoided noticing Mrs Wynter's terror, and his own reaction, as the details of this cruel murder plot were unfolded, was everything I had hoped for: he will be careful, I am confident, never to see or communicate with the woman again. What remained was the question of whether or no Mrs Wynter would call our bluff. For of course it *was* bluff; the wretched Wynter undoubtedly chewed up every fragment of the final, poisonous letter precisely as he had chewed up every fragment of the preceding ones.

As you know, a confession obtained by trickery is not inadmissible in court; but we were aware that in the absence of confirmatory evidence, such a confession would be hopelessly inadequate for the purpose of a prosecution. In any case, we never got it: Mrs Wynter challenged us to produce the sheet of paper which had supposedly been subjected to laboratory examination, and to that challenge we naturally had no reply. For a few moments Mrs Wynter seemed confusedly to suppose that this circumstance would exonerate her in Gellian's eyes. But the signs of her guilt had been too plain; and the two of them left Scotland Yard separately.

Like the majority of policemen I detest murderers, and accordingly it would be no sorrow to me if you were driven to expound Mrs Wynter's guilt in detail in the privileged circumstances of the House of Commons. The Opposition, however, is notoriously solicitous regarding the sensibilities of criminals; consequently I have not doubt that if the truth is made known to them in private they will exert themselves most strenuously to prevent its going further.

Hoping that this letter supplies as much detail as you require,
I am, Sir,
Yours truly,
JOHN KIRKBRIDE

WE KNOW YOU'RE BUSY WRITING,
BUT WE THOUGHT YOU WOULDN'T
MIND IF WE JUST DROPPED IN
FOR A MINUTE

I

"AFTER ALL, IT'S only us," they said.

I must introduce myself.

None of this is going to be read, even, let alone published. Ever.

Nevertheless, there is habit—the habit of putting words together in the most effective order you can think of. There is self-respect, too. That, and habit, make me try to tell this as if it were in fact going to be read.

Which God forbid.

I am forty-seven, unmarried, living alone, a minor crime-fiction writer earning, on average, rather less than £1,000 a year.

I live in Devon.

I live in a small cottage which is isolated, in the sense that there is no one nearer than a quarter of a mile.

I am not, however, at a loss for company.

For one thing, I have a telephone.

I am a hypochondriac, well into the coronary belt. Also, I go in fear of accidents, with broken bones. The telephone is thus a necessity. I can afford only one, so its siting is a matter of great discretion. In the end, it is in the hall, just at the foot of the steep stairs. It is on a shelf only two feet from the floor, so that if I had to crawl to it, it will still be within reach.

If I have my coronary *up*stairs, too bad.

The telephone is for me to use in an emergency. Other people, however, regard it differently.

Take, for example, my bank manager.

"Torhaven 153," I say.

"Hello? Bradley, is that Mr Bradley?"

"Bradley speaking."

"This is Wimpole, Wimpole. Mr Bradley, I have to talk to you."

"Speaking."

"Now, it's like this, Mr Bradley. How soon can we expect some further payments in, Mr Bradley? Payments out, yes, we have plenty of those, but payments in. . . ."

"I'm doing everything I can, Mr Wimpole."

"Everything, yes, everything, but payments in, what is going to be coming in during the next month, Mr Bradley?"

"Quite a lot, I hope."

"Yes, you hope, Mr Bradley, you hope. But what am I going to say to my regional office, Mr Bradley, how am I going to represent the matter to them, to it? You have this accommodation with us, this matter of £500. . . ."

"Had it for years, Mr Wimpole."

"Yes, Mr Bradley, and that is exactly the trouble. You must reduce it, Mr Bradley, reduce it, I say," this lunatic bawls at me.

I can no more reduce my overdraft than I can fly.

I am adequately industrious. I aim to write 2,000 words a day, which would support me in the event that I were able to complete them. But if you live alone you are not, contrary to popular supposition, in a state of unbroken placidity.

Quite the contrary.

I have tried night-work, a consuming yawn to every tap on the typewriter. I have tried early-morning work.

And here H. L. Mencken comes in, suggesting that bad writing is due to bad digestion.

My own digestion is bad at any time, particularly bad during milkmen's hours, and I have never found that I could do much in the dawn. This is a weakness, and I admit it. But apparently it has to be. Work, for me, is thus office hours, nine till five.

I have told everyone about this, begging them, if it isn't a matter of emergency, to get in touch with me in the *evenings*.

Office hours, I tell them, same as everyone else. You wouldn't telephone a solicitor about nothing in particular during his office hours, would you? Well, so why ring me?

I am typing a sentence which starts *His crushed hand, paining him less now, nevertheless gave him a sense of . . .*
     I know what is going to happen after "of": *the appalling frailty of the human body.*
     Or rather, I did know, and it wasn't that. It might have been that (feeble though it is) but for the fact that then the door-bell rang. (I hope that it might have been something better.)

The door-bell rang. It was a Mrs Prance morning, but she hadn't yet arrived, so I answered the door myself, clattering down from the upstairs room where I work. It was the meter-reader. The meter being outside the door, I was at a loss to know why I had to sanction its being scrutinized.
     "A sense of the dreadful agonies," I said to the meter-reader, "of which the human body is capable."
     "Wonderful weather for the time of year."
     "I'll leave you, if you don't mind. I'm a bit busy."
     "Suit yourself," he said, offended.

Then Mrs Prance came.
     Mrs Prance comes three mornings a week. She is slow, and deaf, but she is all I can hope to get, short of winning the Pools.
     She answers the door, but is afraid of the telephone, and consequently never answers that, though I've done my utmost to train her to it.
     She is very anxious that I should know precisely what she is doing in my tatty little cottage, and approve of it.
     "Mr Bradley?"
     "Yes, Mrs Prance?"
     "It's the HI-GLOW."
     "What about it, Mrs Prance?"
     "Pardon?"
     "I said, what about it?"
     "We did ought to change."
     "Yes, well, let's change, by all means."
     "Pardon?"

"I said, Yes."

"Doesn't bring the wood up, not the way it ought to."

"You're the best judge, Mrs Prance."

"Pardon?"

"I'm sorry, Mrs Prance, but I'm working now. We'll talk about it some other time."

"Toffee-nosed," says Mrs Prance.

Gave him a sense of—a sense of—a sense of burr-burr, burr-burr, burr-burr.

Mrs Prance shouts that it's the telephone.

I stumble downstairs and pick the thing up.

"Darling."

"Oh, hello, Chris."

"How are you, darling?"

"A sense of the gross cruelty which filled all history."

"What, darling? What was that you said?"

"Sorry. I was just trying to keep a glass of water balanced on my head."

A tinkle of laughter.

"You're a poppet. Listen, I've a wonderful idea. It's a party. Here in my flat. Today week. You will come, Edward, won't you?"

"Yes, of course, I will, Chris, but may I just remind you about something?"

"What's that, darling?"

"You said you wouldn't ring me up during working hours."

A short silence; then:

"Oh, but *just this once*. It's going to be such a lovely party, darling. You don't mind *just this once*."

"Chris, are you having a coffee break?"

"Yes, darling, and oh God, don't I need it!"

"Well, I'm *not* having a coffee break."

A rather longer silence; then:

"You don't love me any more."

"It's just that I'm trying to get a story written. There's a deadline for it."

"If you don't want to come to the party, all you've got to do is say so."

"I do want to come to the party, but I also want to get on with

earning my living. Seriously, Chris, as it's a week ahead, couldn't you have waited till this evening to ring me?"

A sob.

"I think you're beastly. I think you're utterly, utterly *horrible*."

"Chris."

"And I never want to *see* you again."

. . . a sense of treachery, I typed, sedulously. *The agony still flamed up his arm, but it was now*

The door-bell rang.

—it was now less than—more than—

"It's the laundry, Mr Bradley," Mrs Prance shouted up the stairs to me.

"Coming, Mrs Prance."

I went out on to the small landing. Mrs Prance's great moon-face peered up at me from below.

"Coming Thursday next week," she shouted at me, "because of Good Friday."

"Yes, Mrs Prance, but what has that got to do with *me*? I mean, you'll be here on Wednesday as usual, won't you, to change the sheets?"

"Pardon?"

"Thank you for telling me, Mrs Prance."

One way and another, it was a remarkable Tuesday morning: seven telephone calls, none of them in the least important, eleven people at the door, and Mrs Prance anxious that no scintilla of her efforts should lack my personal verbal approval. I had sat down in front of my typewriter at 9.30. By twelve noon, I had achieved the following:

His crushed hand, paining him less now, nevertheless gave him a sense of treachery, the appalling frailty of the human body, but it was now less than it had been, more than, indifferent to him since, after, because though the paij could be shrugged off the betrayal was a

I make no pretence to be a quick writer, but that really was a very bad morning indeed.

*   *   *

II

Afternoon started better. With some garlic sausage and bread inside me, I ran to another seven paragraphs, unimpeded.

As he clawed his way out, hatred seized him, I tapped out, enthusiastically embarking on the eighth. *No such emotion had ever before*——

The door-bell rang.

—Had ever before disturbed his quiet existence. It was as if——

The door-bell rang again, lengthily, someone leaning on it.

—as if a beast had taken charge, a beast inordinate, insatiable.

The door-bell was now ringing for many seconds at a time, uninterruptedly.

Was this a survival factor, or would it blur his mind? He scarcely knew. One thing was abundantly clear, namely that he was going to have to answer the bloody door-bell.

He did so.

On the doorstep, their car standing in the lane beyond, were a couple in early middle age, who could be seen at a glance to be fresh out from The Duke.

The Duke of Devonshire is my local. When I first moved to this quiet part of Devon, I had nothing against The Duke: it was a small village pub serving small village drinks, with an occasional commercialized pork pie, or sausage-roll. But then it changed hands. A Postgate admirer took over. Hams, game, patties, quail eggs and other such fanciful foods were introduced to a noise of trumpets; esurient lunatics began rolling up in every sort of car, gobble-mad for exotic Ploughman's Lunches and suavely served lobster creams, their throats parched for the vinegar of 1964 clarets or the ullage of the abominable home-brewed beer; and there was no longer any peace for anyone.

In particular, there was no longer any peace for me. "Let's go and see old Ted," people said to one another as they were shooed out of the bar at closing time. "He lives near here."

"Charles," said this man on the doorstep, extending his hand.

The woman with him tittered. She had fluffy hair, and lips so pale that they stood out disconcertingly, like scars, against her blotched complexion. "It's Ted, lovey," she said.

"Ted, of course it's Ted. Known him for years. How are you, Charley boy?"

"*Ted,* angel."

I recognized them both, slightly, from one or two parties. They were presumably a married couple, but not married for long, if offensive nonsenses like "angel" were to be believed.

"We're not interrupting anything," she said.

Interested by this statement of fact, I found spouting up in my pharynx the reply, "Yes, you sodding well are." But this had to be choked back; bourgeois education forbids such replies, other than euphemistically.

"Come on in," I said.

They came on in.

I took them into the downstairs living-room, which lack of money has left a ghost of its original intention. There are two armchairs, a chesterfield, a coffee-table, a corner cupboard for drinks: but all, despite HI-GLOW, dull and tattered on the plain carpet.

I got them settled on the chesterfield.

"Coffee?" I suggested.

But this seemed not to be what was wanted.

"You haven't got a drink, old boy?" the man said.

"Stanislas," the girl said.

"Yes, of course. Whisky? Gin? Sherry?"

"Oh, Stanislas darling, you are *awful,*" said this female. "Fancy asking."

I had no recollection of the name of either of them, but surely Stanislas couldn't be right. "Stanislas?" I asked.

"It's private," she said, taking one of his hands in one of hers, and wringing it. "You don't mind? It's sort of a joke. It's private between us."

"I see. Well, what would you like to drink?"

He chose whisky, she gin and Italian.

"If you'll excuse me, I'll have to go upstairs for a minute," I said, after serving them.

One thing was abundantly clear: Giorgio's map had been wrong, and as a consequence——

"Ooh-hooh!"

I went out on to the landing.

"Yes?"

"We're lonely."

"Down in just a minute."

"You're doing that nasty writing."

"No, just checking something."

"We heard the typewriter. Do come down, Charles, Edward I mean, we've got something terribly, terribly important to tell you."

"Coming straight away," I said, my mind full of Giorgio's map.

I refilled their glasses.

"You're Diana," I said to her.

"Daphne," she squeaked.

"Yes, of course, Daphne. Drink all right?"

She took a great swallow of it, and so was unable to speak for fear of vomiting. Stanislas roused himself to fill the conversational gap.

"How's the old writing, then?"

"Going along well."

"Mad Martians, eh? Don't read that sort of thing myself, I'm afraid, too busy with biography and history. Has Daphne told you?"

"No. Told me what?"

"About Us, old boy, about Us."

This was the first indication I'd had that they *weren't* a married couple. Fond locutions survive courtship by God knows how many years, fossilizing to automatic gabble, and so are no guide to actual relationships. But in "Us", the capital letter, audible anyway, flag-wags something new.

"Ah-ha!" I said.

With an effort, Stanislas leaned forward. "Daphne's husband is a beast," he said, enunciating distinctly.

"Giorgio's map," I said. "Defective."

"A mere brute. So she's going to throw in her lot with me."

Satisfied, he fell back on to the cushions. "Darling," he said.

As a consequence, we were two miles south-west of our expected position. "So what is the expected position?" I asked.

"We're eloping," Daphne said.

"This very day. Darling."

"Angel."

"Yes, this very day," said Stanislas, ostentatiously sucking up the last drops from the bottom of his glass. "This very day as ever is. We've planned it," he confided.

The plan had gone wrong, had gone rotten. Giorgio had failed.

"Had gone rotten," I said, hoping I might just possibly remember the phrase when this pair of lunatics had taken themselves off.

"Rotten is the word for that bastard," said Stanislas. Suddenly his eyes filled with alcoholic tears. "What Daphne has suffered, no one will ever know," he gulped. "There's even been . . . beating." Daphne lowered her lids demurely, in tacit confirmation. "So we're off and away together," said Stanislas, recovering slightly. "A new life. Abroad. A new humane relationship."

But was his failure final? Wasn't there still a chance?

"If you'll excuse me," I said, "I shall have to go upstairs again."

But this attempt aborted. Daphne seized me so violently by the wrist, as I was on the move, that I had difficulty in not falling over sideways.

"You're with us, aren't you?" she breathed.

"Oh yes, of course."

"My husband would come after us, if he knew."

"A good thing he doesn't know, then."

"But he'll guess. He'll guess it's Stanislas."

"I suppose so."

"You don't mind us being here, Charles, do you? We have to wait till dark."

"Well, actually, there is a bit of work I ought to be getting on with."

"I'm sorry, Ted," she said, smoothing her skirt. "We've been inconsiderate. We must go." She went on picking at her hemline, but there was no tensing of the leg muscles, preliminary to rising, so I refilled her glass. "No, don't go," I said, the British middle class confronting its finest hour. "Tell me more about it."

"Stanislas."

"H'm, h'm."

"Wake *up*, sweetie-pie. Tell Charles all about it."

Stanislas got himself approximately upright. "All about what?"

"About Us, angel."

But the devil of it was, if Giorgio's map was wrong, our chances had receded to nil.

"To nil," I said. "Nil."

"Not nil at all, old boy," Stanislas said. "And as a matter of fact, if you don't mind my saying so, I rather resent the 'nil'. We may not be special, like writer blokes like you, but we aren't 'nil', Daphne and me. We're human, and so forth. Cut us and we bleed, and that. I'm no great cop, I'll grant you that, but Daphne—Daphne——"

"A splendid girl," I said.

"Yes, you say that now, but what would you have said five minutes ago? Eh? Eh?"

"The same thing, of course."

"You think you're rather marvellous, don't you? You think you've . . . got it made. Well, let me tell you one thing, Mr so-called Bradley: you may think you're very clever, with all this writing of Westerns and so on, but I can tell you, there are more important things in life than Westerns. I don't suppose you'll understand about it, but there's Love. Daphne and I, we love one another. You can jeer, and you do jeer. All I can tell you is, you're wrong as can be Daphne and I, we're going off together, and to hell with people who . . . jeer."

"Have another drink."

"Well, thanks, I don't mind if I do."

They stayed for four whole hours.

Somewhere in the middle, they made a pretence of drinking tea. Some time after that, they expressed concern at the length of time they had stayed—without, however, giving any sign of leaving. I gathered, as Giorgio and his map faded inexorably from my mind, that their elopement plans were dependent on darkness: this, rather than the charm of my company, was what they were waiting for. Meanwhile, with my deadline irrevocably lost, I listened to their soul-searching—he unjustifiably divorced, she tied to a brutish lout who unfortunately wielded influence over a large range of local and national affairs, and would pursue her to the ends of the earth unless precautions were taken to foil him.

I heard a good deal about their precautions, registering them without, at the time, realizing how useful they were going to be.

"Charles, Edward."
   "Yes?"
   "We've been bastards."
   "Of course not."
   "We haven't been letting you get on with your work."
   "Too late now."
   "Not really too late," lachrymosely. "You go and write, and we'll just sit here, and do no harm to a soul."
   "I've rather forgotten what I was saying, and in any case I've missed the last post."
   "Oh, Charles, Charles, you shame us. We abase ourselves."
   "No need for that."
   "*Naturally* we abase ourselves. We've drunk your liquor, we've sat on your . . . your sofa, we've stopped you working. Sweetie-pie, isn't that true? Haven't we stopped him working?"
   "If you say so, sweetie-pie."
   "I most certainly do say so. And it's a disgrace."
   "So we're disgraced, Poppet. *Bad*," she said histrionically. "But are we so bad? I mean, he's self-employed, he's got all the time in the world, he can work just whenever he likes. Not like you and me. He's got it *made*."
   "Oh God," I mumbled.
   "Well, that's true," Stanislas said, with difficulty. "And it's a nice quiet life."
   "Quiet, that's it."
   "Don't have to do anything if you don't want to. Ah, come the day."
   "He's looking cross."
   "What's that? Old Charles looking cross? Angel, you're mistaken. Don't you believe it. Not cross, Charles are you?"
   "We *have* stayed rather long, darling. Darling, are you awake? I say, we *have* stayed rather long."
   "H'm."
   "But it's special. Edward, it's special. You do see that, don't you? Special. Because of Stanislas and me."

I said, "All I know is that I . . ."

"Just this once," she said. "You'll forgive us just this once? After all, you *are* a free agent. And after all, it's only us."

I stared at them.

I looked at him, nine-tenths asleep. I looked at her, half asleep. I thought what a life they were going to have if they eloped together.

But "It's only us" had triggered something off.

I remember that on just that one day, not an extraordinary one, there had been Mrs Prance, the meter-reader, Chris (twice: she had telephoned a second time during working hours to apologize for telephoning the first time during working hours), the laundry-man, the grocer (no Chivers Peas this week), my tax accountant, a woman collecting for the Church, a Frenchman wanting to know if he was on the right road to The Duke.

I remembered that a frippet had come from the National Insurance, or whatever the hell it's called now, to ask what I was doing about Mrs Prance, and if not, why not. I remembered a long, inconclusive telephone call from someone's secretary at the BBC—the someone, despite his anxiety to be in touch with me, having vanished without notice into the BBC Club. I remembered that undergraduates at the University of Essex were wanting me to give them a talk, and were going to be so good as to pay second-class rail fare, though no fee.

I remembered that my whole morning's work had been a single, botched, incomplete paragraph, and that my afternoon's work, before this further interruption, had been little more than 200 words.

I remembered that I had missed the post.

I remembered that I had missed the post before, for much the same reasons, and that publishers are unenthusiastic about writers who keep failing to meet deadlines.

I remembered that I was very short of money, and that sitting giving drink to almost total strangers for four hours on end wasn't the best way of improving the situation.

I remembered.

I saw red.

A red mist swam before his eyes, doing the butterfly stroke.

I picked up the poker from the fireplace, and went round behind them.

Did they—I sometimes ask myself—wonder what I could possibly be doing, edging round the back of the chesterfield with a great lump of iron in my hand?

They were probably too far gone to wonder.

In any case, they weren't left wondering for long.

III

Eighteen months have passed.

At the end of the first week, a detective constable came to see me. His name was Ellis. He was thin to the point of emaciation, and seemed, despite his youth, permanently depressed. He was in plain clothes.

He told me that their names were Daphne Fiddler and Clarence Oates.

"Now, sir, we've looked into this matter and we understand that you didn't know this lady and gentleman at all well."

"I'd just met them once or twice."

"They came here, though, that Tuesday afternoon."

"Yes, but they'd been booted out of the pub. People often come here because they've been booted out of the pub."

Lounging on the chesterfield, ignoring the blotches, Ellis said, "They were looking for a drink, eh?"

"Yes, they did seem to be doing that."

"I'm not disturbing your work, sir, I hope."

"Yes, you are, Officer, as a matter of fact. So did they."

"If you wouldn't mind, sir, don't call me 'Officer'. I am one technically. But as a mode of address it's pointless."

"Sorry."

"I'll have to disturb your work a little bit more still, sir, I'm afraid. Now, if I may ask, did this . . . this *pair* say anything to you about their plans?"

"Did they say anything to anyone else?"

"Yes, Mr Bradley, to about half the population of South Devon."

"Well, I can tell you what they said to me. They said they were going to get a boat from Torquay to Jersey, and then a plane from

Jersey to Guernsey, and then a Hovercraft from Guernsey to France. They were going to go over to France on day passes, but they were going to carry their passports with them, and cash sewn into the linings of their clothes. Then they were going on from France to some other country, where they could get jobs without a *permis de séjour*."

"Some countries, there's loop-holes as big as camels' gates," said Ellis, biblically.

I said, "They'll make a mess of it, you know."

"Hash-slinging for her," said Ellis despondently, "and driving a taxi for him. What was the last you saw of them?"

"They drove off."

"Yes, but when?"

"Oh, after dark. Perhaps seven. What happened to them after that?"

"The Falls."

"Sorry?"

"The *Falls*. Their car was found abandoned there."

"Oh."

"No luggage in it."

"Oh."

"So presumably they got on the Torquay bus."

"You can't find out?"

Ellis wriggled on the cushions. "Driver's an idiot. Doesn't see or hear *anything*."

"I was out at the Falls myself."

"Pardon?"

"I say, I was out at the Falls myself. I followed them on foot—though of course, I didn't *know* I was doing that."

"Did you see their car there?" Ellis asked.

"I saw several cars, but they all look alike nowadays. And they all had their lights off. You don't go around peering into cars at the Falls which have their lights off."

"And then, sir?"

"I just walked back. It's a fairly normal walk for me in the evenings, after I've eaten. I mean, it's a walk I quite often take."

(And I had, in fact, walked back by the lanes as usual, resisting the temptation to skulk across the fields. Good for me to have dumped the car un-noticed near the bus-stop, and good for me to have remembered about the luggage before I set out.)

"Good for me," I said.

"Pardon?"

"Good for me to be able to do that walk, still."

Ellis unfolded himself, getting up from the chesterfield. Good for me that he hadn't got a kit with him to test the blotches.

"It's just a routine inquiry, Mr Bradley," he said faintly, his vitality seemingly at a low ebb. "Mrs Fiddler's husband, Mr Oates's ex-wife, they felt they should inquire. Missing Persons, you see. But just between ourselves," he added, his voice livening momentarily, "they neither of 'em care a button. It's obvious what's happened, and they neither of 'em care a button. Least said, Mr Bradley, soonest mended."

He went.

I should feel guilty; but in fact, I feel purged.

Catharsis.

Am I purged of pity? I hope not. I feel pity for Daphne and Stanislas, at the same time as irritation at their unconscionable folly.

Purged of fear?

Well, in an odd sort of way, yes.

Things have got worse for me. The strain of reducing my overdraft by £250 has left me with Mrs Prance only two days a week, and, rather more importantly, I now have to count the tins of baked beans and the loaves I shall use for toasting.

But I feel better.

The interruptions are no less than before. Wimpole, Chris, my tax accountant all help to fill my working hours, in the same old way.

But now I feel almost indulgent towards them. Towards everyone, even Mrs Prance.

For one thing, I garden a lot.

I get a fair number of flowers, but this is more luck than judgement. Vegetables are my chief thing.

And this autumn, the cabbages have done particularly well. Harvest cabbages, they stand up straight and conical, their dark green outer leaves folded close, moisture-globed, protecting firm, crisp hearts.

For harvest cabbages, you can't beat nicely rotted organic fertilizers.

Can I ever bring myself to cut my harvest cabbages, and eat them?

At the *moment* I don't want to eat my harvest cabbages. But I dare say in the end I shall.

After all, it's only them.

CASH ON DELIVERY

MAX LINSTER WAS degenerate in the stricter sense of the word: I mean that he really had had something substantial—education; a good heredity; a stable, by no means poverty-stricken background—to degenerate from. He was aware, therefore, that his errand was very exceptional: so far as Linster knew, this was the first time that an Englishman, in England, had hired another man to commit murder for him since the case of Ley and Smith. That occasion had ended badly; but for a fee of two or three hundred pounds, what could you expect? Linster's own fee was going to be twenty times larger—and he had every reason to believe that Smith's fate, the being hanged by the neck until he was dead, would never, never be his.

The house bulked large in front of him as he slipped in through the side gate. In the distance a church clock struck ten—and fleetingly, Linster frowned. He had twenty minutes to work in, or at the very utmost half an hour; for at midnight a certain private plane would be taking off for the Continent from a lonely field in Norfolk, and whatever else happened, Linster, who had cogent motives for not using any of the more conventional modes of transport, was going to be on that plane; he had no intention of relying on a second chance which might never come. Whether he succeeded in this last job in England would consequently depend a good deal on the organization at this end. . . .

He reconnoitred, glancing in circumspectly at the lighted, uncurtained window of the servants' sitting-room; then went and located the first-floor window to which—through certain intermediaries—he had been directed. To reach its balcony proved no way difficult; and the french windows, he found, had been left unfastened, as promised. Inside, he deduced his surroundings with his nose. A woman's bedroom. This was it, all right.

In accordance with his instructions, he waited; and presently, hearing footsteps approaching along the corridor, moved swiftly and silently across the room to station himself behind the door. It opened slowly. A switch clicked; light flooded down from the crystal electrolier . . .

And Ley came into the room.

Only this man was much younger than Ley—probably not more than thirty-five or so. His thinning, crinkled blond hair gleamed under the electric bulbs; his face was puffy and sullen; the right arm of his dinner-jacket was empty, pinned neatly to his breast. From behind him, as he stood peering sharply about, "Mr Elliston?" Linster murmured.

Jacob Elliston swung round abruptly, teetering on his heels. And stared . . .

"So," he breathed, relaxing his scrutiny at last. "So . . . You're who they sent."

Linster nodded. "I'm who they sent."

Turning from him, Elliston pushed the door to and crossed the room to close the curtains. He said:

"Let's not waste any time . . . As you'll have gathered, this is my wife's bedroom. At the immediate moment, my wife is downstairs with her brother, who came over for the evening. But in the next few minutes, he'll have to leave to catch his train. She'll come up to bed."

Linster's eyes flickered, and he glanced at his watch; but for the moment he had no comment to offer.

"After that," Elliston went on, facing him again, "it'll be up to you. But you must understand that you'll get no money if you don't succeed in actually . . ."

"In actually killing the lady," suggested Linster with a smile. "Yes, I understand that, Mr Elliston. Cash strictly on delivery." He stepped forward—watchfully, for this was the first really crucial stage in the tactics he had planned: unlike one or two men whom he had met, and others he had heard of, Linster had no interest in murder for its own sake; so if robbery would achieve the same end . . . "But you have the money ready, I hope," he said.

The muzzle of Elliston's pistol halted him when there was still some distance between them. And Elliston shook his head.

"No," he said. "Don't try that. The money's ready, certainly, but for the time being it's in my bedroom safe. If you want it, you'll have to do the job as specified."

"Of course." Linster remained unperturbed. "I never considered anything else. Incidentally, there were one or two details . . ."

"You are to use both your hands."

"Yes." Linster's gaze strayed to the empty sleeve. "Yes. Very sensible. They go a lot by the bruises."

"And also you're to fake a burglary. Force the windowcatch. Mess the room up a bit . . . Yes, and you'd better take that jewel-box away with you. For your information, there's nothing very valuable in it. But as it's locked, you're not to know that, are you?"

Still holding the pistol in steady alignment, Elliston moved towards the door. "I'm going now—to my own bedroom, where I shall turn the radio on loud." He opened the door a fraction and paused, listening. "That's my brother-in-law leaving now. My wife has had a tiring day: she'll be coming up almost at once. So if I return here with the money in, say, twenty minutes . . ."

"Twenty minutes," said Linster, "should be fine."

And so Elliston left, and soon the sound of a dance band blared out from a room near by. Linster, meanwhile, had been appraising his surroundings. The window curtains were useless to him, he saw, for they barely reached the ground; he had no intention of grovelling under any bed, and the floor of the wardrobe was cluttered up with shoes. That left either a clothes cupboard set into the wall, or else the space behind the door—and without more than a minimal hesitation, Linster chose the former. It was true that once inside it, you had no means of seeing what was going on; but at least you could *hear* . . . . Flexing his fingers inside his gloves, Linster switched off the lights and vanished like a shadow.

When Joséphine Demessieux entered her mistress's bedroom that evening she was in her usual bad temper. The pretty, callow, inexperienced provincial French girl whose coming to England to work, two years before, had seemed such an adventure, was long since extinct. From the way she was overpaid, Joséphine had correctly deduced herself indispensable: in servant-starved England there was always another job waiting, so why trouble yourself about giving value for money? Moreover, the Elliston household was a wealthy one—so that quite soon sharp envy had joined irresponsibility in hastening the deterioration of Joséphine's character. Madame could be considerate, to be sure; just now, for instance, when she had decided to walk with her brother to the railway-station, she had said that Joséphine need not wait up. But that was nothing; what was important was that the mistress possessed beautiful things while the maid had none. . . .

So Joséphine performed her few small duties in the bedroom with a slovenly rapidity; and then, lingering, succumbed in Madame's fortunate absence to the most ancient and inevitable servant-peccadillo of them all, the trying-on of her employer's envied belongings. The ring, and the brooch, and the mink cape worn over her plain black dress, transformed her; by the time Linster—judging his victim to be now sufficiently relaxed, and conscious that in any case the span remaining to him was too short to allow of further inaction—by the time Linster slipped out from the cupboard, Joséphine was as fine a lady as ever in her wildest dreams she had hoped to be. . . .

Moving noiselessly up behind her, Linster watched her face reflected in the mirror before which she was pirouetting. He was still a foot or two away from her when she saw him and turned—but his left hand was broad and quick, and her throat slender. Thumb on the one side, middle finger on the other, found, and tightened on, the carotid and the vagus nerve. So Joséphine Demessieux uttered no cry or other sound, and indeed was unconscious for a whole minute, or even more, before at last her lungs burst, and she died. . . .

Linster lowered the body carefully to the floor; then took the folded counterpane, and with it covered the thing that he had done. To break the window-catch, to pull out drawers and disarrange their contents, was the work of only a very few minutes. The little jewel-box, after brief consideration, he threw out of sight under the bed. When Elliston re-entered the room, pistol again in hand, Linster was nowhere to be seen; but he emerged at once from his concealment on seeing who the intruder was.

For all his earlier self-assurance, Elliston was sweating now; his eyes, as he stared at the huddled shape under the counterpane, looked almost blind. He said:

"It—it's done."

Linster nodded. "It's done."

"You're certain she's. . . "

"Yes, Mr Elliston, she's quite dead." Linster stooped, pulled a flaccid white hand from under the counterpane. "If you don't believe me, feel this."

But Elliston jerked backwards, shuddering. "That ring," he mumbled presently, still staring as if hypnotised. "It's one she hardly ever——"

Linster straightened up, dropping the hand. He said: "The money, Mr Elliston. Five thousand."

In silence the packets of notes changed hands. "So I'll be leaving you now, Mr Elliston," said Linster when he had stowed them away; and as a malicious afterthought: "Sorry I can't stay to make a pass at that nice little maid your wife has. But that's life."

Elliston's white, uncomprehending face turned slowly. "The—the maid?"

"The maid. I looked in at the window of your servants' sitting-room before I climbed up here, and there she was. Dark. A soft-looking mouth. Quite a girl. I'd recognize *her* again, anywhere. But"—shrugging—"I had this urgent appointment. And you don't ever get the money till you've delivered the goods—some sort of goods. And a man must live."

Elliston was gazing blankly at him. He said: "I don't understand what you're talking about."

But Linster, with one leg already over the edge of the balcony, only shook his head.

"You will, Mr Elliston," he said pleasantly. "You will."

SHOT IN THE DARK

IN A ROOM high up in a corner of New Scotland Yard, Detective Inspector Humbleby turned to his visitor and said "Look here, Gervase, if you'd like to go on ahead. . . ."

"No, no, no." From the depths of an armchair, Gervase Fen gestured dissent. "I'm quite happy as I am. But what exactly is this telephone call we're waiting for? Anything interesting?"

"The case it's concerned with is interesting in some ways," said Humbleby. "I was assigned to it when the Chief Constable of Wessex asked us for help. I've been working on it with a local CID man called Bolsover. It's him I'm expecting to hear from—just a routine report until such time as I can get back down there again.

"Cassibury Bardwell, the place is called. It's a sort of hybrid—too big to be a village and too small to be a town. In the countryside round about there are, apart from the farms, a few remote, inaccessible little cottages, and one of these was occupied, until he was killed last Saturday evening, by a young man named Joshua Ledlow.

"Here is this Joshua, then, thirty years old, unmarried, and of a rather sombre and savage temperament. He is looked after by his sister Cicely, who shows no particular fondness for him and would in any case prefer to be looking after a husband, but who remains unwooed and, having no fortune of her own, housekeeps for Joshua as a respectable substitute for earning a living.

"Joshua, meanwhile, is courting, the object of his fancy being a heavily-built girl called Vashti Winterbourne. He has a rival, by name Arthur Penge, by vocation the local ironmonger; and it is clear that Vashti will soon have to make up her mind which of these suitors she is going to marry.

"In the meantime, relations between the two men degenerate into something like open hostility, the situation being complicated latterly by the fact that Joshua's sister Cicely has fallen in love with Penge, thereby converting the original triangle into a sort of—um—quad-rangle. So there you have all the ingredients for a thoroughly explosive mixture—and in due course it does in fact explode.

"With that much preliminary I can go on to describe what happened last Saturday and Sunday. What happened on Saturday was a public quarrel, of epic proportions, between Joshua, Cicely and Penge. This enormous row took place in the entrance-hall of a pub called The Jolly Ploughboy, and consisted of (a) Penge telling Joshua to lay off Vashti, (b) Cicely telling Penge to lay off Vashti and take her, Cicely, to wife instead, (c) Penge telling Cicely that no man not demonstrably insane would ever dream of marrying her and (d) Joshua telling Penge that if he didn't keep away from Vashti in future, he, Joshua, would have much pleasure in slitting his, Penge's, throat for him.

"Note, please, that this quarrel was quite certainly genuine. I mention the point because Bolsover and I wasted a good deal of energy investigating the possibility that Penge and Cicely were somehow in cahoots together—that the quarrel so far as they were concerned was a fake. However, the witnesses we questioned weren't having any of that; they told us roundly that if Cicely was acting they were Dutchmen, and we were forced to believe them.

"No chance of collusion in that department, then. Mind you, I'm not saying that if Penge had visited Cicely afterwards and abased himself and asked her to marry him, she mightn't have forgiven him. But the established fact is that between the quarrel and the murder next day he definitely didn't visit her or communicate with her in any way. With the exception of a single interlude of one hour (and of the half-hour during which he must have been committing the crime), his movements are completely accounted for from the moment of the quarrel up to midnight on the Sunday; and during that one hour, when he might (for all we know) have gone to make his apologies to the woman, she was occupied with entertaining two visitors who can swear that he never came near her.

"The next event of any consequence was on Sunday morning, when Cicely broke her ankle. The effect of this accident was, of course, to immobilize her and hence, in the event, to free her from any possible suspicion of having herself murdered her brother Joshua, since his body was found some considerable distance away from their cottage.

"The crime was discovered at about ten o'clock that evening, by several people in a party; the scene being a little-frequented footpath on the direct route between Joshua's cottage and the centre of Cassibury.

"There was only one substantial clue; I mean the revolver, which Bolsover found shoved into the hedge a little distance away with a fine set of prints on it. Working along the usual lines, we soon uncovered the existence of the Penge-Joshua-Vashti triangle. And so it didn't take us long to ascertain that the prints on the gun were the prints of Arthur Penge.

"When eventually he was asked to explain this circumstance, he told a demonstrable lie: saying that he'd handled the gun three days previously when Joshua (of all people) had brought it into his ironmonger's shop to ask if a crack in the butt could be repaired. On its being pointed out to him that Joshua had quite certainly been in Dorchester during the whole of the day mentioned, and so couldn't possibly have visited the Cassibury ironmonger's, he wavered and started contradicting himself and eventually shut up altogether, in which oyster-like condition he's been ever since—and very wise of him, too.

"However, I'm anticipating; we didn't ask him about the gun until after we'd gone into the problem of the time of Joshua's death. The medical verdict was too vague to be helpful. But then two women came forward to tell us that they'd seen Joshua alive at seven, when they'd visited the cottage to condole with Cicely. So clearly the next thing to do was to talk to Cicely herself.

"It turned out that by a great stroke of luck she hadn't heard of the murder yet; the reasons for this being (a) the fact that Joshua had planned to be away from home that night in any case, so that his absence had not alarmed her, and (b) the fact that the local sergeant, a temperamentally secretive person, had sworn everyone who knew of the murder to silence. Consequently, Bolsover was able to put his most important questions to Cicely before telling her his reason for asking them—and a good thing, too, because she had a fit of the horrors as soon as she heard her brother was dead, and the doctor's refused to allow her to talk to anyone since.

"Anyway, her testimony was that Joshua left the cottage at about 8.15 on the Sunday evening (a quarter of an hour or so after her own visitors had gone), with a view to walking into

Cassibury and catching a bus to Dorchester. And that meant that he could hardly have reached the spot where he was killed much earlier than a quarter to nine.

"So the next thing was to find out where Penge had been all the evening. And what it amounted to was that there were two periods of his time not vouched for by independent witnesses—the period from seven to eight (which didn't concern us) and the period from 8.30 to nine. Well, the latter, of course, fitted beautifully; and when we heard that he'd actually been seen, at about a quarter to nine, close to the place where the murder was committed, we started getting the warrant out.

"And that was the point at which the entire case fell to pieces.

"Penge had lied about his whereabouts between 8.30 and nine; we knew that. What we *didn't* know was that from 8.20 onwards two couples were making love no more than a few feet away from the place of the murder, and that not one of those four people heard a shot.

"And so that, as they say, was that. Penge certainly shot Joshua. But he didn't do it between 8.30 and nine. And unless Cicely was lying in order to help him—which is inconceivable—he didn't do it between seven and eight, either."

There was a long silence when Humbleby finished speaking. Presently Fen said: "Well then, the situation, as I understand it, must be that it isn't Penge who has the alibi. It's the corpse."

"The *corpse*?"

"Why not? If Cicely was lying about the time Joshua left the cottage—if, in fact, he left much earlier—then Penge could have killed him between seven and eight."

"But I've already explained——"

"That it's inconceivable she'd lie on Penge's behalf. I quite agree. But mightn't she lie on her brother's? Suppose that Joshua, with a revolver in his pocket, is setting out to commit a crime. And suppose he tells Cicely, if any questions are asked, to swear he left her much later than, in fact, he did. And suppose that a policeman questions Cicely on this point before she learns that it's her brother, and not the man he set out to kill, who is dead. Wouldn't that account for it all?"

"You mean——"

"I mean that Joshua intended to murder Penge, his rival in this young woman's affections; that he arranged for his sister (whom

Penge had just humiliated publicly) to give him, if necessary, a simple alibi; and that in the event Penge struggled with Joshua, got hold of the gun and killed his assailant in self-defence. Behold him, then, with a water-tight alibi created—charming irony—by his enemy."

Shatteringly, the telephone rang, and Humbleby snatched it from the cradle. "Yes," he said. "Yes, put him on. . . . Bolsover?" A long pause. "Oh, you've seen that, have you? So have I—though only just. . . . Allowed to talk to people again, yes, so you—WHAT?" And with this squeak of mingled rage and astonishment Humbleby fell abruptly silent, listening while the telephone crackled despairingly at his ear. When at last he rang off, his round face was a painter's allegory of gloom.

"Bolsover thought of it, too," he said sombrely. "But not soon enough. By the time he got to Cicely's bedside, Penge had been there for hours. They're going to get married: Cicely and Penge, I mean. She's forgiven him about the quarrel. And, of course, she's sticking to her story about the time Joshua left the house. Very definite about it, Bolsover says. In the interests of justice——"

"Justice?" Fen reached for his hat. "I shouldn't worry too much about that, if I were you. A marriage based on mistrust and evasion will be a worse punishment, in the long run, than anything the Old Bailey could do. The mills of God, you know: where Penge and Cicely are concerned I should imagine they'll grind very, very small indeed. . . ."

THE MISCHIEF DONE

"PEOPLE ARE SUPERSTITIOUS about diamonds," said Detective Inspector Humbleby. "They believe all sorts of extraordinary things. And of course diamonds do give us a lot of trouble at the Yard, one way and another."

" 'O Diamond! Diamond!' " his host said.

"Is that a quotation? No, no, don't bother, leave it. Among the many delusions people have about diamonds——"

" 'O Diamond! Diamond! Thou little knowest the mischief done!' " Out of the depths of the armchair in his rooms in St Christopher's, Gervase Fen, University Professor of English Language and Literature, reached across with the decanter to pour more sherry into his guest's glass. "Allegedly said by Isaac Newton," he explained. "His dog Diamond knocked over a candle and incinerated 'the almost finished labours of some years' ."

"Mathematicians oughtn't to keep dogs," said Humbleby. "And historians oughtn't to lend their manuscripts to John Stuart Mill." He presumably meant Carlyle, part of whose *French Revolution* was used as kindling by Mill's housemaid. "*Rubies* are more valuable than diamonds," Humbleby obstinately went on. "And contrary to popular supposition, diamonds are very brittle. You can lose hundreds of pounds by just dropping one on a carpet."

"Humbleby, what is all this about?"

And Humbleby, deflated, sighed. "I've been made a fool of," he said. "Somebody went and stole an enormous great valuable diamond literally from under my nose, when I was supposed to be helping to protect it."

"That's bad."

"Not that the owner's lost it, mind."

"That's good."

"He's just hidden it somewhere, or rather, his brother has. The whole thing's an insurance fraud," said Humbleby aggrievedly.

"We know it's that, but unfortunately we can't begin to prove it . . . I don't enjoy being made a fool of."

"No one does."

"I should like somehow to get a bit of my own back."

"Naturally, naturally."

"So can you help me, do you think?"

"I very much doubt it," said Fen. "But tell me what happened, and I'll try."

"The diamond's owner," said Humbleby, "was—and if I'm right about the business, still effectually is—a Soho jeweller called Asa Braham. Years ago he had a robbery, a genuine one, and I was put in charge of the investigation, and it went on for rather a long time, so I got to know Asa quite well. He's a wiry little man with frizzy black hair, fiftyish, very lively, very active; a charmer, and sharp-witted with it. I never exactly trusted him, but I did get to like him—and that was why I stupidly allowed myself to get involved in this business of the *Reine des Odalisques*."

"Who on earth is she?"

"That's what the diamond's called. Its first owner, who christened it, was a Frenchman—apparently," said Humbleby waspishly, "a man of very little judgement, taste or even ordinary good sense. Anyway, it was from him that Asa Braham bought the thing, about six weeks ago now, for well over £100,000."

"Good grief."

"Yes, it was a lot, but although it was only mined quite recently it's become one of the famous diamonds. And Asa wanted it like mad, though he couldn't really afford it. You see, he's one of those jewellers who get obsessed with stones for their own sake—not at all a good thing from the commercial point of view (and in fact, Asa, though he's done adequately well, has never really flourished), but I suppose it has its satisfactions, even if I can't begin to imagine them myself. Asa passionately wanted that diamond; he *had* to have it; and he mortgaged himself to the hilt to pay the price. God alone knows what, apart from crime, he expected to do next. There he was with the *Reine*, doting on it, and nothing, psychologically, would have suited him better than to spend hours staring at the wretched bauble every day for the rest of his natural life. Yet if he'd actually settled down to that, he'd have been made bankrupt in a year or less. What I mean is that he just couldn't *afford* to keep the thing. Considered simply as a buy, the whole transaction was crazy: it isn't at all easy to dispose of hugely valuable stones even for what they cost, let alone at a profit; you may have to wait for years."

"Fairly clear so far," said Fen. "You seem to have deviated, though. What about this earlier robbery? Genuine, you say?"

"Oh yes, definitely. We got the villains eventually, and put them away. Also, we got back some of the stones. On the rest, the insurance company paid—reluctantly."

"Yes, they're always reluctant."

"In this case, they were specially so. They didn't think Asa's precautions were good enough. But, God, jewellers," said Humbleby with some feeling. "I'll tell you what jewellers do: they roam about in dark alleys, at dead of night, with small fortunes rattling loose in their waistcoat pockets . . . For the stones Asa didn't recover, as I said, the company paid. But the word went round that he was slack, and after that his insurance contracts were much stiffer, not just in terms of premiums but in terms of security too. So—he bought the *Reine*, and naturally he insured it, but there were a great many specific conditions. I've seen that contract—after the theft of the *Reine*, of course I was working in with the insurance company—and it's very tightly drawn indeed, as regards how the stone was looked after.

"So there you have it: the diamond bought about six weeks ago, and first carefully stowed away in the vault of Asa's shop, and then when four weeks ago Asa had to go off to Brazil on business, it was transferred to the safe deposit at Pratt's Bank in Portland Square."

"Was that so very much safer, then?"

"The insurance company, Krafft International, certainly thought it was, at any rate for as long as Asa was out of the country. So Asa dutifully took it along there, with a safeguard, the day before he left."

"What safeguard?"

"Not what, who: a man from the Safeguard security corps. It was a condition of Asa's insurance contract that a Safeguard man had to be with the *Reine* whenever it wasn't actually under lock and key."

Humbleby wriggled back into his chair and sipped his drink. "So far, so good," he presently went on. "And what happened next was that a week ago Asa arrived back at London Docks on the *Luis Pizarro*—like me, he's terrified of aeroplanes, so he travelled both ways by sea—and rang me up the moment he got on shore, and asked me if I was free to come along with him and his precious diamond and the contractual Safeguard man on a trip to his cottage in Dorset, where he was scheduled to show the diamond off to a possible purchaser. Well, I didn't all that much want to go, but on the other hand the Yard's a terrible place nowadays, full of great grinning oafs who've never read a book for pleasure in their lives, and I get away from it whenever I possibly can. So here was an excuse of sorts, and I took it."

"Yes, I can understand that all right," said Fen. "But what did he want you *for*? I mean, what did he *say*?"

"He said it'd be nice to see me again, and he was sure I'd like to have a look at the diamond."

"And you believed that?"

"Well, not entirely," said Humbleby. "I thought there was probably something a bit funny going on. But that, you see, was all the more reason why I should be there. Only unfortunately, as it turned out, I wasn't quite suspicious enough. Anyway, I went.

"I went, and we met at Pratt's Bank. Asa came there direct from the docks—and by the way, there's absolutely no doubt about that: since the thing happened, we've checked and double-checked all of his movements, backwards, forwards and inside out, and he certainly had no time for any tricky business between getting off the boat and meeting me. I was the first to get to Pratt's. Then the Safeguard man arrived, a menacing figure called Shirtcliff. Last came Asa, full of the joys of spring. And I didn't like that. He was too cheerful altogether, for a man besotted with a diamond who's on the way to losing it to a customer after only a few weeks' ownership. He needed a customer, yes, and he was lucky to get one. Even so, he ought to have been just a bit glum about it, not completely cock-a-hoop.

"Asa went down into the vaults, and Shirtcliff and I went with him as far as the system allowed, which wasn't, of course, the whole way. However, he was out again in a couple of minutes or less, waving a quite large black velvet jewel-box; and he handed this to Shirtcliff; and Shirtcliff took a look inside it, and grunted affirmatively, and shut the box up again, and put it in his briefcase; and we all went upstairs again, and out of the bank, and round the corner to where a self-drive hired car was waiting; and in that Asa drove us down to Stickwater in Dorset, me sitting beside him in the front passenger seat, and Shirtcliff in the back glowering and clutching his brief-case with the diamond in it.

"Our next consideration must be Asa's brother Ben."

"Isn't this narrative becoming rather mannered, Humbleby?" said Fen restively. "And by the way, is it going to turn out that there's some question of paste's having been substituted for the real thing?"

"No, it isn't. That doesn't arise at all."

"I see. Well, when is something going to happen?"

"In a moment, in a moment. Ben first. Ben is younger than his brother Asa, and much bigger and tougher. He's also the dependent one of the pair—did at one time have a jeweller's business of his own, but he was no good at it and it went bust. Since then he's lived off Asa, and also lived *with* Asa, either in their flat in London, or else in this dismal little house in Dorset. Ben looks after the domestic side, in so far as it gets looked after at all. They're neither of them married, and they do without servants, and they live together in a sort of devoted squalor.

"Envisage, then," said Humbleby dramatically, "this car—a puce Cortina, I ought perhaps to add—driving down from London to Stickwater in Dorset, Asa Braham at the wheel, myself beside him, the man Shirtcliff in the back, the diamond——"

"Humbleby, haven't you told me all this already?" Fen was more fretful than ever. "And come to that, is something portentous or significant going to happen on this drive, something relevant, I mean, to what you seem to be trying to start out to describe to me?"

"Come to *that*," said Humbleby a shade aggrievedly, "aren't you being unduly particular? All I'm trying to do is give you the atmosphere, the ambient, the whole——"

"Yes, granted, and very nice too, but my point is that the drive itself——"

"It admittedly wasn't important." Forced to this concession, Humbleby busied himself with finding and lighting a cheroot. "Asa talked a good deal, but then, he always does, not just on drives, but on every occasion, everywhere. So at last, without incident, we arrived."

"At last."

"Not at any sort of gracious little country seat, but at a tiny, extraordinarily unprepossessing, example of Victorian farmhouse architecture, subsequently transformed, at no very evident expense, into a small dwelling-house. It was very isolated, with grounds which were, I suppose, fairly extensive, but horribly unkempt. As to the house itself, that really amounted to little more than two up, two down, with kitchen and bath: all dispiritingly grey and damp and obviously uncared-for. Ben Braham opened the front door for us, and seemed—I have to say 'seemed'—in an evil temper. He took us into the front room right, a tattered sort of living-room, and offered us a drink. There was thereupon a row. The only drinks actually available, it turned out, were either home-brewed beer, made years before from some sort of chemist's kit, or a rather small amount of a dreadful Italian apéritif called Casca Oli. Ben was supposed to have got drink in, but for some reason (perhaps to give cogency to his being on bad terms with his brother Asa) hadn't in fact done so. He was supposed to have done a lot of things, including, in response to a radiogram from the *Luis Pizarro*, coming down earlier in the day to 'open the house up'. Well, he was there, all right, but that was about the most you could say. 'I've packed my bag,' he told us—and in fact there was a suitcase of some description hanging about in the hall outside—'and you know what I'm going to do? I'm going to go back to London and have myself a bloody great piss-up.'

"This announcement apparently didn't strike Asa favourably, giving rise, indeed, to a prolonged spell of angry fraternal shouting and counter-shouting. Even so, I stayed suspicious, as the words flew round and about my head. Meanwhile, the egregious Shirtcliff—who'd refused both Casca Oli and home-brewed beer, apparently more on principle than because they were equally odious—continued to nurse the *Reine des Odalisques* in its fat jewel-box in his briefcase on his lap.

"So there we all four of us were, in this awful living-room, sipping ullage while a row went on. And now, to make a fifth, the potential customer for the *Reine* arrived. You've heard of Clyde Savitt?"

"The film star."

"Yes."

"He buys diamonds for his wife."

"Yes: like Richard Burton—though perhaps on not quite so massive a scale."

"And he's an expert on diamonds, isn't he?"

"Yes—again like Burton, I suppose, up to a point. But with Savitt there's an extra dimension. Savitt *père* was a jeweller, and Savitt *fils*, before he went into pictures, was intended to become one too. So before the lures of the old ciné trapped him, he learned a lot, about diamonds particularly. In short, he'd be pretty nearly impossible to deceive. He wanted the *Reine* for his wife; he knew it, from its many photographs; and when he eventually *saw* it . . ."

Humbleby sucked at his cheroot, long and deep. "We went," he said, "into the room on the other side of the little hallway. That is, all of us did except Ben, who was still—and again I have to say 'apparently'—sulking. Savitt, I gathered, was resting between pictures at a modest country house conveniently close by. He had come to Asa, rather than the other way round, because he didn't want his wife to know anything at all in advance about this possible jewel transaction. It was all perfectly plausible, and perfectly plain.

"What was less plausible, and certainly less immediately plain, was why we'd made the move from the one room to the other at all. (I can see the reasons now, of course, but then, hindsight's a wonderful thing.) Asa's notion was that in the living-room where we'd all started off, Savitt included, the light wasn't adequate, or at any rate, not adequate for examining a diamond. But this deficiency, though certainly real enough, didn't seem to be much remedied when we got to Asa's 'study', which had in its ceiling a bulb of very low wattage indeed, so much so that although it was a small room, and we were crowded together, we could barely make out the expressions on each other's faces . . . I must now," said Humbleby with some dignity, "describe this room to you."

"Yes, yes, of course."

"Small, then. And not what you'd call overfurnished, either. There was a round table, at about the middle. There was a minute flat-topped desk with nothing on it. There was an almost equally exiguous old-fashioned safe—completely empty, it subsequently transpired. There were a crack-springed armchair, and a desk chair. And finally, in one corner, you could see a huddle of old

Casca Oli cartons, with a couple of Anglepoise lamps and a few other odd bits and pieces. No pictures, and only one window, and that had steel shutters over it, closed and locked. By way of making light conversation, Asa explained that they'd been closed and locked for years, he having lost the only key. The shutters had been put in, he said, at a time when he'd been in the habit of bringing stones down to Stickwater, until finally the insurance companies had said, to his great.grief, that he mustn't do it any longer. Also from earlier, less stringent days dated the safe, and the admittedly pretty solid door—much more solid, as we found to our cost, than any of the others in the house—which we'd come in by.

"Light, Asa said: we must have, he said, like the dying Goethe, more light; and he started fussing with the two Anglepoises, neither of which, it soon became clear, was fitted with a plug in any way corresponding with the one socket in the room's skirting-board. (By now, I need hardly tell you, my suspicions were very serious indeed. But even so, how was *I* to know what was planned, what was in fact just about to happen?) Anyway, there it was: Asa fatuously muttering about adaptors, Ben presumably still in the living-room (or possibly already off, with his prepared suitcase, for his projected piss-up in London); Clyde Savitt, the unlucky Shirtcliff and my almost equally unlucky self hovering around Asa in this dreadful little room, waiting for inchoate possibilities to congeal into some sort of event. This they almost immediately did, but not before Clyde Savitt, tiring like the rest of us of Asa's busy fumblings with flexes, suggested that we might perfectly well have a preliminary look at the *Reine* straight away. And Asa was all for this. Leaving the Anglepoises, he gave instructions to Shirtcliff. And with the air of a man acting insufferably against his better judgement, Shirtcliff took the jewel-box from his briefcase, placed it in the middle of the round table and retired angrily to stand with his back against the super-special door, which we'd closed after us. Shirtcliff had already inspected, and found sound, the steel window-shutters; now he was adopting what even a much more intelligent man would of course have thought the best general defensive position available.

"He was wrong about that, but really, one can scarcely blame him.

"Jewel-box on table, then; and Asa advances on it, opens it reverently and stands gazing at its contents, even under that impossibly dim illumination, with the pride of a Mrs Worthington whose daughter has not only gone on the stage, but unaccountably made a spectacular success of the business. As to Clyde Savitt, whose behaviour up to this point had been impeccable, excitement overcame him. He snatched the *Reine* out of the box (Shirtcliff stiffening visibly), snatched a loupe from his pocket and stood there making his examination in a breathless silence which affected all of us.

"Then he said, 'Yes: that's it, all right.'

"I mention this crucial remark not to criticize its civility, nor even to suggest that diamond-mad people go diamond-mad whenever they see a diamond, to the exclusion of absolutely everything else. I mention it because it was *true*. You said something earlier about the possibility of paste. But Savitt was sure then, and is sure now, that what he had in his hand was the *Reine* and nothing but the *Reine*—and this in spite of the awful light and the unfortunate circumstances generally.

"Savitt said, 'Yes: that's it, all right. And I want to buy it.' And he put it back in its box, rather quickly, as if it was burning his fingers.

"And then suddenly we were in complete darkness."

Humbleby shook his head, not in negation but sadly. An efficient officer, he was consequently finding his own part in these proceedings disagreeable to recall.

"Looking back on it," he said, "I remember, or imagine I remember, the click of the mains switch. This, along with the meter and so forth, was in the hallway immediately outside the study. And it was this, certainly, that was used. So there we were, in chaos and old night, with the little gleam of the diamond in its open jewel-box on the round table our only illumination of any sort. By then it was blackness outside the house—no moon or stars; and even if it hadn't been, the steel shutters over the window would have cut out any light absolutely.

"Then the door burst open (no light at all from the hallway outside), and someone came tearing into the room, and the gleam of the diamond winked out, and the someone ran off again, and the door slammed, shutting us in; and the footsteps went away, out of the front door, and crunched quickly along the drive out of earshot; and somewhat distantly, a car engine started and revved up, and then that was gone too.

"From the moment of the light going out to the moment of the intruder nipping off again, and slamming the door, was, I suppose, scarcely more than three seconds. Enough, though, for the *Reine* to be gone.

"Shirtcliff had been bashed in the small of the back by the door opening, and had gone sprawling. Even so, he was the first to recover. But it was hopeless. Thanks to Asa's precautions, the room door had a Yale on it; and the intruder had reversed the snib as he rushed in; so all he had to do when he left was click the door shut and reverse the snib on the outer side (there exist, unfortunately, Yales with this double arrangement).

"And we were trapped."

Again shaking his head, "We were trapped," said Humbleby, "for close on two hours. I know this must seem nearly incredible, but you must remember those shutters, and also the fact that there was no telephone, and also the fact that apart from my cigarette-lighter, which was by no means inexhaustible, we couldn't see a bloody thing we were doing. Of course we shouted, and we banged. But Ben, it appeared, the only other person in the house, had long since left, plus suitcase, for his mafficking in London. That, anyway, was his story, when it came to the crunch: he'd gone off almost straight away after we moved from the living-room to the study. And this never was, nor could be, disproved. Me, I never believed it for a moment. I was as sure as could be that it was Ben who'd turned off the mains switch, careered into the room, nabbed the diamond and whisked off out again, all with the happy collaboration of his brother Asa. But proving that was, and is, something else again. Shirtcliff could have had an accomplice, or even, come to that, Clyde Savitt. What, at that stage, did we know? What *could* we know?

"I'm fairly good at locks, but there were no tools—apart from scraps of Anglepoises which Shirtcliff tore apart with his bare hands—so as I've said, it was nearly two hours before we got that door open at last. Hanging on to Shirtcliff's sleeve, with the lighter guttering in my hand, I hauled him outside, turned the mains switch back on and then hauled him back inside again.

" 'Strip!' I said.

"To do him justice, he saw the point, and he stripped at once. I went over his discarded clothes very carefully, and then, equally carefully, I went over *him*. (We're supposed, at the Yard, to have read a lot of books about such things, and I can distinctly remember glancing through one or two of the least offensive of them.) Asa, who was putting on a great act of shock and horror, at this stage started bellowing about bodily orifices, but as I pointed out to him, not just the diamond had disappeared from the study, but a bloody great jewel-case as well. Bodily orifices, I pointed out to Asa, were very unlikely receptacles for that. And in fact the jewel-case was eventually found, thrown away at the side of the drive, only a few yards from the front door. By that time, it was, I need hardly say, empty.

"Shirtcliff—'clean'—ran off to a telephone with instructions from me. Meanwhile, I myself went over the study with what writers inexperienced in hyphenation call a fine tooth-comb, and which——"

"Humbleby, listen a moment. It——"

"—and which, I can assure you, brought nothing whatever, of any relevance, to light. I also searched Savitt and Asa, and they searched me. Still nothing. And there could be nothing. Someone had burst in, and grabbed the *Reine* in its box, and disappeared again, and that was all there was to it. Still, I *had* to take all the precautions, I *had* to do the searching—just in case. But nothing. I was very scrupulous about it all, and I can assure you—nothing, then or afterwards."

Fen stared at his guest with more than usual attention: he had found the tale, if not exactly brilliant, at any rate an interesting one. "And finally?" he prompted.

"Finally, Ben Braham was stopped in his car by the police at Deare, getting on for 80 miles from Stickwater, two-and-a-half hours' drive. No diamond on him or in him, of course, and no diamond anywhere in the car. How could there have been? Eighty miles! At any point, at his leisure, knowing perfectly well how appallingly we were trapped back at that loathsome little house, he could have turned off the London road into a lane, stopped at a field-gate, gone into the field, poked a hole with his finger in the bank, injected the diamond, covered it up, made a careful note of the place (he had a torch in his car, but that doesn't prove anyone guilty of anything) and then simply traipsed back and driven on again. He could, and can, simply return and pick the miserable little object up again whenever it suits him."

"Which won't be yet."

"No, of course not yet: probably not for a long time. Not, anyway, until a long time after Krafft has paid out the insurance money. Ben and Asa will know, in any case, that we shall be keeping an eye on them for a bit. They won't make any move until they're completely certain it won't backfire in the form of a Conspiracy to Defraud charge."

"And when they do at last make their move to pick up the diamond," said Fen: "what then? Does Asa Braham get it anonymously through the post from a conscience-stricken thief?"

"Lord, no." And Humbleby smiled, with some affection, at his host, whom it was pleasing to find, for the moment, almost as dim-witted as he, Humbleby, had throughout the whole Braham business felt himself to be. "Because in that case, you see, the insurance money would have to be repaid, and Asa wouldn't be able to afford that. But it'll be reward enough, for Asa, just to have the *Reine* back and be able to gloat over it secretly. As I've told you, he's crazy about stones. And that, I suppose, has been the basis of the whole trouble."

Fen thought for a bit. Then he said mildly, "Superstitions about diamonds. You started by talking about those—but you don't, if I may say so, seem to be altogether free from them yourself."

"I know practically everything about diamonds," said Humbleby, with some indignation. "Diamonds, now——"

"Yes, of course. But you say that when the lights went out —and there was no sort of reflected light—this particular diamond shone in the dark."

"Yes, certainly it did. Diamonds are self-luminescent. Look up any book on the subject and you'll find——"

"No, I shan't. Sorry, Humbleby, but not for the circumstances *you've* described. Diamonds do shine in the dark, yes. But they don't produce light, like glow-worms. They store it and reproduce it. For a diamond to shine in the dark, it must have been subjected to light first—fairly bright light, and fairly recently.

"But what sort of light had your precious *Reine des Odalisques* been under? Well, if the tales are true, it'd been for three weeks in the darkness of a bank's safe-deposit vault; then a man called Shirtcliff glanced at it for a moment, in ordinary daylight; finally, it was exposed to a low-wattage bulb for what doesn't sound like much more than two minutes, though I suppose——"

"*Less* than two minutes." Humbleby struck his brow, with his clenched fist, in a transpontine manner which was nevertheless patently sincere. "God, what an imbecile I've been! You mean, Asa was so infatuated with the thing that he took it with him to South America."

"Yes, that seems likely."

"And then marched into Pratt's Bank with it in his pocket, and then simply popped it into the jewel-box which he *had* left there, and brought it out again."

"Almost certain, I'd say. The diamond had stored all that light because he was staring at it virtually up to the last possible moment. Either he'd forgotten that when Ben put their plan into operation the diamond would shine, or else—which seems more likely—he just thought that the interval, between the light going out and the *Reine* being grabbed, would be too short for anyone to notice."

"Well, *I* noticed," said Humbleby. "The question is, did Savitt? Did Shirtcliff? If they both did"—and here an unhealthy revengeful gleam appeared in Humbleby's eye—"Asa's claim on Krafft Insurance isn't going to look too good."

"If he disgracefully neglected a specified precaution, then the whole thing is void."

"Void."

"And did only Asa have access to that Pratt's Bank safe-deposit? I mean, if he could just give the key to someone else, then he could say—"

"No, it had to be him. Couldn't be anyone else."

And here Fen considered Humbleby with a faint air of displeasure which, except between such old friends, might have seemed slightly ungracious. "I don't altogether dislike the sound of your Asa," he said. "Of course, it's bad to try to defraud insurance companies, and if for all of you that diamond did in fact shine in the dark, then . . . Even so, there are some moods"—and here, Fen brought the sherry out again—"in which it's possible to feel that the thing was worth a try."

*   *   *

"Asa withdrew his claim," said Humbleby when six months later he and Fen met coincidentally at the Travellers', "because Savitt and Shirtcliff had both, like me, glimpsed the *Reine* self-luminescing. So the claim wouldn't wash—and now, I understand, Asa's quite a poor man. He makes out, though, as poor men so often mysteriously do. Is your conscience at rest?"

"Shirtcliff?"

"Sacked from Safeguard for incompetence, and at once taken on by the Metropolitan Police."

"Savitt?"

"Richer and more famous and more courteous than ever."

"The diamond?"

"Well . . . Somewhere. I suppose we'll never know."

They never did know, but at the last, one man, without knowing it, knew.

Police Constable Bowker's "manor" was centred on the hamlet of Amble Harrowby, a focus for much rich agricultural activity. Left-wing himself, Bowker was unable to suppress at least a theoretical distaste for the local Socialist peer, Lord Levin, whose notional egalitarianism had somehow never prevented him from enjoying such benefits as an inherited title, with additional tremendous inherited wealth, could bestow. At the same time, Bowker realized that in this respect he was perhaps being a little naïve, the more so as Lord Levin went to such particular trouble to be pleasant to everyone, Bowker himself by no means excluded. There could scarcely—Bowker reflected, as he buzzed through the lanes in his white crash-helmet, on his little machine—be a more agreeably conscienceless man in the entire land.

In particular, this scheme of a trout-lake was good. Lord Levin had many farm tenancies on his property; one of these—always notable for the combined age, idleness and incapacity of its tenant—had recently been caused to be vacated by death; and Lord Levin was taking the opportunity of converting some fifteen acres of notoriously unproductive land into a fairly large-scale water for fishing.

Now, Police Constable Bowker, whatever his general feelings about Lord Levin, didn't at all disapprove of this. On the contrary, since the lake was to be a natural-seeming sort, confluent with the surrounding mild bulges of the countryside, he felt, and felt quite strongly, that here was an instance where private riches might quite well redound to the public good.

He stopped his machine, therefore, at a specially good point of vantage—Copeman's Rise—from which the lake-making proceedings, which had by now been going on for a good two weeks, could be unusually well viewed.

Immense scars, bulldozer-induced, lay across the land. Hedgerows had been ripped up and tossed aside. Tons of unsifted earth were being lorry-laden and whipped off to unknown dumping-grounds. The whole spectacle—admittedly for the moment hideous, but still, Bowker felt, marginally better than the grubby little contraceptive-infested copses it was replacing—was one of massive alteration and change. Bowker's heart warmed. Soon, all this unavoidable scooping-out would give way to a placid expanse of brownish waters (Bowker's romanticism would have preferred bluish, but his practicality forbade this), lightly ruffled by the prevailing winds.

So far, so good. But as Bowker came to a halt, it became evident to him that his emotions regarding this presently tormented landscape, so soon to be converted to beauty, were not entirely shared. Two men, who had parked their shabby car close by, were having to support each other, arms round shoulders, in order to contemplate the scene with equanimity.

Bowker thought that he perhaps recognized them. They were a jeweller and his brother with a country cottage at Stickwater, fifteen miles away. Bowker also thought that they were possibly supporting one another because they were drunk.

But then he shifted a little nearer—and decided he had been wrong about that.

Bowker went back to his machine, re-started the engine, gunned it up and headed for the London road. There are some things even a country copper thinks it best not to interfere with: and one is when he sees two male adults watching a trout-lake being made with great scalding tears pouring down their cheeks.

MERRY-GO-ROUND

"No," SAID Detective Inspector Humbleby. "No, it doesn't really do to play jokes on the police. You're liable to get yourself into serious trouble, for one thing. And for another, it's essentially unfair. . . .

"However, there has been just one instance, quite recently, of the thing's being brought off with impunity and, on the whole, justification." He chuckled suddenly. "I don't think anything's given us so much simple pleasure at the Yard since Chief Inspector Noddy tripped over his sword and fell headlong at the Investiture last year. . . . Tell me, did you ever come across a DI called Snodgrass?"

Gervase Fen said that he was sorry, he had not.

"I thought you might have done, for the reason that Snodgrass is our expert on literary forgeries. . . . However. The thing about him is that although he's undoubtedly a very good man at his job, he's far from being an amiable character.

"Not to put too fine a point on it, Snodgrass is dour and suspicious to a quite offensive degree. And with decidedly Left-wing political views, too. So that when he came to deal with Brixham——"

"Brixham the newspaper baron?"

"Yes. Though it was Brixham the book-collector whom Snodgrass offended. Brixham specializes in the Augustan period, you know—Pope and Addison and all that lot. That's relevant to what follows, in the sense that Brixham would obviously know a great deal about the pitfalls of literary forgery and would be in a position, with his money and printing-presses and laboratories and so forth, to turn out a very creditable forgery himself.

"He must have had accomplices, of course—technicians of various sorts. But Snodgrass never succeeded in getting a line on them, and it's evident that Brixham secured their secrecy by the simple process of letting them into the joke.

"Well now, the origin of it all was five years ago, when trouble arose over a first edition which Brixham had sold to a fellow-collector, and which was suspected to be a forgery.

"Snodgrass investigated. And in the course of his investigations he was quite needlessly uncivil to Brixham (who turned out in the end to be completely innocent)—uncivil enough to have justified a strong complaint to the AC, if Brixham had chosen to make it. He didn't choose, however. He had other ideas.

"And just six months ago, after a long interval of patient preparation, those ideas came to fruition.

"What happened was that an old boy called Withers (who I think must have been a party to the plot) came to the Yard asserting that a letter recently sold him by Brixham was faked. The sum involved was only a pound or two. But if the letter was a fake, and Brixham knew it, then unquestionably a fraud had been committed. And accordingly Snodgrass started to enquire into the matter with a fervour worthy, as they say, of a better cause.

"The letter was dated 9 August 1716, and purported to be written by one Thomas Groate. You've heard, of course, of the publisher Edmund Curll?"

Fen nodded. "The man of whom Arbuthnot said that his biographies had added a new terror to death."

"Just so. Well, this Groate was apparently a clerk of Curll's. Nothing is known of him except that he was once alive and kicking. And no authenticated specimens of his handwriting remain. His letter—the one Brixham sold to Withers—consisted of petty gossip about the publishing world of his time. And its only real interest lay in a scabrous and, I should think, patently untrue anecdote about the poet Pope.

"Now, it'd be wearisome if I were to detail all the tests Snodgrass applied to this document. As you know, there are a good many these days—constitution, size, cutting, creasing and watermark of the paper; constitution of the ink, and the chemical changes brought about in it by ageing; whether the writing overlays or underlays stains and mould-marks; style of calligraphy, spellings, accuracy of topical reference; provenance; and so on and so forth. What with ultra-violet and spectroscopy and all those things, the ordinary forger doesn't have much chance.

"But Brixham wasn't an ordinary forger. And it was only when Snodgrass came to consider the pen with which the letter had been written that he at last struck oil. For the letter had been written with a steel pen. And so far as is known, the first steel pens weren't produced till about 1780.

"Snodgrass ought to have paused at this point, and considered. Of all the mistakes which Brixham might have made in faking such a letter, this was one of the least likely. And if Snodgrass hadn't been so furiously intent on convicting Brixham, he must have realized that the mistake was a deliberate one.

"He didn't realize, however. Triumphantly he confronted Brixham with the proof of his fraud. And what should Brixham do, after hearing him out, but suddenly 'remember' that he had in his possession an advertising handbill of the period, in which, among other things, the advertiser (one Wotton) called the public's attention to his new steel pens, never before made, and of sovereign advantage. . . .

"Baffled, Snodgrass returned with the handbill to the Yard.

"Once again the machinery was put into operation. And once again every test failed excepting one.

"This time it was a matter of the advertiser's address. The paper of the handbill was watermarked 1715, and the address was given as Bear Hole Passage, Fleet Street. But reference to a historical gazetteer revealed the fact that on the accession of the Tories to power, in 1714, Bear Hole Passage was renamed Walpole Lane. So if the advertiser didn't know his own address. . . .

"For the second time Snodgrass confronted Brixham with the proof of his forgery. And for the second time Brixham 'happened' to have an answer.

"On this occasion it was a letter purporting to be written by the publisher Lintot, in which reference was made in passing to the fact that the stationer Wotton, a convinced Whig, 'doth obstinately and childishly refuse to employ the new address'—or words to that effect. In short, Wotton would seem, judging from Lintot's letter, to have done much what Mr Bevan would probably do if the Post Office insisted on renaming his house Winston Villa.

"I think that at this stage Snodgrass must have begun to suspect that he was being made a fool of. But by now he was too deeply involved to draw back. Again all possible tests were made. Again they all failed excepting one. That one disclosed a radical oversight, certainly: the handwriting of the Lintot letter, shaky and uneven, did not correspond at all with the handwriting of letters known to have been written by Lintot. . . .

"But that was just what finished it, you see."

"Finished it?" Fen was surprised. "It's a glorious trick as far as it goes, of course. But I've been wondering all along how it could be artistically rounded off. How did the Lintot handwriting finish it?"

Humbleby laughed delightedly. "It finished it because one of the bits of gossip in the forgery that started the chain—the letter from the clerk Groate—was that the publisher Lintot had recently had a slight stroke, 'which hath altered his hand almost beyond recognising'.

"So you see, Snodgrass couldn't prove the Groate letter a forgery until he'd proved the Wotton handbill a forgery. And he couldn't prove the Wotton handbill a forgery until he'd proved the Lintot letter a forgery. And he couldn't prove the Lintot letter a forgery until he'd proved the Groate letter a forgery. . . ."

Humbleby reached for his beer. "Withers's cheque which he'd paid for the Groate letter was returned to him by Brixham. Some doubt had arisen, said Brixham in a covering letter, regarding the document's authenticity. As to Snodgrass, he was granted extended sick-leave, and is now away on a cruise." Humbleby shook his head. "But we're afraid—or perhaps I should say we hope—that he'll never be the same man again."

OCCUPATIONAL RISK

IT WAS NEARLY half-past two by the time Detective Inspector Humbleby arrived at The Grapes. Weaving his way across the upstairs dining-room, he slumped down in a chair beside a tall, lean man who was drinking coffee at a table by a window.

"Sorry about this," said Humbleby. "And now that I *am* here, I'm afraid I can't stop for more than a few minutes." He ordered sandwiches and a pint of bitter. "You got my message all right?"

"Oh yes." The tall man, whose name was Gervase Fen, nodded cheerfully enough as he lit a fresh cigarette. " 'Detained on official business.' Anything interesting?"

Humbleby grunted. "In some ways. But chiefly it's *awkward*. Am I to let a certain eminent professional man catch the evening plane to Rome, or am I not? That's my problem. There isn't really enough evidence to justify my holding him here. But then for that matter, there's not much evidence of *any* sort, so far. . . .

"You see it's like this. . . . Late yesterday afternoon there was a burial in the churchyard of St Simeon's, in Belgravia. At the time, the grave was only half filled in; but they did, of course, leave a fair amount of earth covering the coffin—so that when the sexton went along early this morning to finish the job, dropped his pipe out of his waistcoat pocket into the hole, clambered down to get it, and felt his foot strike wood, he decided he'd better investigate.

"Underneath the coffin he found the naked body of a man, which it's obvious must have been dumped there—and a very good hiding-place, too—under cover of last night's fog. The man was thin, elderly, distinguished-looking. He'd been killed by a violent blow on the back of the head. His dentures were gone, and there were no obvious identifying marks on his body. In due course he was taken to the nearest police station.

"And there, for the second time, chance took a hand. One of the sergeants, a reliable man called Redditch, recognized this corpse as someone he'd talked to in a pub near Victoria early yesterday evening.

"Redditch—a plain-clothes officer—was going off duty at the time, and had stepped in for the odd pint on his way home. The stranger was sitting alone at one of the tables, Redditch says, drinking brandy and scribbling music of some sort on a scrap of music MS paper. There was no other seat free, so Redditch settled down beside him. . . .

"And presently they got into conversation.

"The conversation to start with was general. Redditch mentioned that he was thinking of having a fishing holiday in the West Country, and the old gentleman recommended a particular inn in Devonshire. He wrote it down for Redditch. His pockets were full of odd bits of paper, Redditch says, and he tore the top off one of these and wrote the address on the back." Humbleby groped in his pocket. "Here's what he wrote. It's been tested for prints, so. . . ."

He handed the sliver of paper across to Fen, who examined it pensively. On one side, written in pencil in a large and sloping but none the less educated hand, was the legend "Angler's Rest Hotel, Yeopool, nr Barnstaple"; on the other, in the same calligraphy, a fragment which ran: ". . . ving . . . hysterical fugues wh . . .".

"A music critic?" Fen suggested, as he passed this tenuous piece of evidence back.

"We think it's obvious he must have been some sort of musician, yes."

"A musician, or else. . . ." Fen hesitated. "I say, Humbleby, what was Redditch's impression of the man? I mean, how did he size him up?"

"Well, as *cultivated*, certainly," said Humbleby. "Cultivated, retiring, not rich but decidedly respectable, honest, dignified —and in spite of the education, a rather simple and unsophisticated mind where worldly matters were concerned. Also not, Redditch thinks, at all a practised drinker. Which is just as well. Because but for the fact that this kindly, respectable old party was knocking back brandy without, apparently, any clear conception of what it was likely to do to him, we'd probably never have known where to begin to look for his murderer. The brandy went to his head, you see, and he became suddenly confiding. He was up from the country—Redditch had already

gathered that much. Now, moved by alcohol and moral indignation, he fell abruptly to telling Redditch why.

"Some eight months previously, it seemed, the old gentleman
had taken on a servant girl, a stranger to his part of the world, to
help look after him. She appears to have been a pleasant straight-
forward creature, and her employer soon became very fond of
her, in what Redditch is quite sure was a genuinely paternal way.
Presently, however, the signs of this girl's pregnancy became too
plain to ignore. The old gentleman wasn't at all the sort to turn
her out of his house on that account; on the contrary, as she had
no relations to go to, he was quite agreeable to her having the
child on his premises. . . . But if he wasn't angry with the girl, he
was certainly angry with her seducer. The girl refused, obstinately, to name this person. But then, in bearing the child, she
died—and her employer, going through her belongings after her
death, found a letter which enabled him to identify the guilty
party with a virtual certainty. A knight, he told Redditch: a
knight, and an eminent professional man, and pretty well off:
definitely *not* the sort of person who ought to be allowed to
wriggle out of his responsibilities in the matter. Our man wrote to
this knight, saying as much. He got no reply. Whereupon, full of
dignified fury, he had determined to come to London to attend to
the business in person.

"And this, he told Redditch in conclusion, he was now about to
do. He had telephoned the guilty party on arrival, and had made
an appointment to meet him in the evening at his flat, when he
proposed to confront him with the incriminating letter and
demand that he shoulder his liabilities. . . . At this, Redditch felt
a twinge of uneasiness, he says. Eminent professional men, with a
position to keep up in the world, are not really at all likely to
welcome stern old gentlemen who are resolved to bring their
illegitimate babies home to roost with them. However, there was
nothing that Redditch could do about it, except ask the name of
the man this old gentleman was going to visit; and that the old
gentleman firmly declined to give. With his tale told, he asked
Redditch the way to Harcutt Terrace in Westminster; said
goodbye; went out into the fog; and as far as we know, was never
seen alive by anyone, other than his murderer, again."

Humbleby gulped his beer and sighed. "It's evident, then, that
Redditch's forebodings were justified. And the situation we're

left with is that we have three suspects from Harcutt Terrace—Sir George Dyland, the banker; Sir Sydney Cockshott, the psychiatrist; and Sir Richard Pelling, the barrister—without, however, anything at all to indicate which of them is likely to be our man. They're all of them coming along to the Yard some time this afternoon to look at the body (though if any of them identifies it I shall be very surprised indeed); and one of them—as I mentioned earlier—wants to go off subsequently to a conference in Rome. Should I let him? *I* don't know. If I could just find *some* indication that one of the three was to be preferred, as a suspect, to the others. . . ."

Fen considered; then he said: "Are you intending to give them the background? To tell them about Redditch, and all that?"

"I'm not intending to tell them a single thing," replied Humbleby with emphasis, "until I have a very much clearer idea of where we stand."

"M'm," said Fen. "In that case, you know, there's a simple little trap that you could try. Admittedly there's only one chance in three of its working. But if it doesn't work, I can't see that any harm will be done, and if it does you'll know whom to concentrate on. . . .

"Like this: show them that scrap of paper the old gentleman gave to Redditch, and ask each of them to make a quick guess at the writer's occupation. Ask them to make alternative guesses if you feel like it, but don't *labour* the business too much: don't let them brood over it for *minutes*, I mean. If you do that——"

Humbleby was staring. "But look, Gervase, it's surely obvious what they'll all say. What good——"

"Is it?" Fen chuckled. "Still, for old times' sake, do try it none the less. And ring me at the United University as soon as you have their answers. I'll be there all afternoon. . . . "

In fact, the call came through at about 4.30.

"They said," said Humbleby, who sounded annoyed, "just exactly what you'd expect them to say: namely, that the person who had written on that scrap of paper was presumably a musician or a music critic of some kind. *All* of them said that."

"No alternative guesses?"

"None."

"And which," Fen asked, "is the one who wants to go to

Rome?" Humbleby told him. "Let him go, then," said Fen. "*He* isn't your man. Quite obviously, from what we know, your man is——"

"You see," Fen went on, "the phrase 'hysterical fugues', though it *could* be music criticism—and in the case of your old gentleman undoubtedly was—has in addition a much simpler connotation: in psychiatry and medicine, an hysterical fugue is a certain type of amnesia. That being so, your psychiatrist ought at least to have had an *alternative* guess at the writer's occupation, if he really *was* guessing, and not speaking from knowledge. His carelessness in suggesting just music must, I think, mean that he already *knew* the writer's occupation. And if he already knew that, then patently he'd *recognized the handwriting....*

"None of which is hanging evidence, of course: you'll have to delve for that. But as a working hypothesis I should say it was fairly sound—wouldn't you?"

DOG IN THE NIGHT-TIME

GERVASE FEN, Professor of English Language and Literature in the University of Oxford, found Ann Cargill waiting for him in his rooms in college when he returned there from dinner at the George on a certain bitter February evening.

She was a quiet, good-looking girl, the most pleasant, if not the brightest, of the few undergraduates to whom he gave private tuition.

"Nice to see you back," he said. For he knew that Ann's father had recently died, and that she had been given leave of absence for the first few weeks of term in order to cope with the situation and its aftermath.

"It's not about work, I'm afraid," she confessed. "Not altogether, I mean. I—I was wondering if you could help me over something—something personal."

"Surely your moral tutor——" Fen began, and then suddenly remembered who Ann's moral tutor was. "No," he said. "No, of course not . . . Wait while I get us some drinks, and then you can tell me all about it."

"I'm probably being several sorts of a fool," said Ann, as soon as they were settled with glasses in their hands. "But here goes, anyway . . . I don't know if you know anything about my family, but my mother died years ago. I'm an only child, and my father—well, the important thing about him, for the moment, is that he had a passion for jewels.

"Jewels weren't his business. They were his hobby. And two or three months ago he sank an enormous amount of money —about three-quarters of his capital, I should think—into buying a single diamond that he'd set his heart on, a huge thing, quite flawless.

"Well, now, at the beginning of this year Daddy shut up our house at Abingdon—I live on my own in the vacs, you see, in a flat in Town; he liked me to do that—and flew out to Australia on business. He didn't take the diamond with him. It was left in the house——"

Fen lifted his eyebrows.

"Ah, yes, but the point is, it was really quite as safe there as it would have been in the bank. At the time he started collecting jewels Daddy had his study made as near burglar-proof as money could buy; and there was only one set of keys to the door and the safe; and when he went to Australia he left those with Mr Spottiswoode, his solicitor."

Ann took a deep breath. "And then he—he was killed. In a street accident in Sydney . . . I—I went down to Abingdon after the wire came, and wandered about there a bit. Remembering. That was when I saw Mr Spottiswoode, the solicitor, driving away from the house.

"I don't think he saw me. I called after him, but he didn't stop. And, of course, being Daddy's executor, he had a perfect right to be there. But I always hated Mr Spottiswoode. . . ."

Ann wriggled in her chair. "And I'm pretty sure," she added, "that he was a crook."

After a brief pause: "I've no proof of that," she went on. "And you don't have to believe it if you don't want to. I only mentioned it because it's one of the reasons why I've come to you. Mr Spottiswoode——"

"You say he 'was' a crook."

"Yes, that's the next thing. Mr Spottiswoode's dead, you see. He died three weeks ago, very soon after I saw him at Abingdon; quite suddenly of a heart attack. And at that stage he hadn't yet got what they call a grant of probate of Daddy's will.

"So that what's happened since, is that my Uncle Harry, who's now my legal guardian, has been made administrator of the estate on my behalf. In other words, Mr Spottiswoode *did* have the keys to Daddy's study, and Uncle Harry has them *now*."

"And is Uncle Harry a crook too?"

Ann wriggled still more. "I know it must sound as if I've got some hellish great neurosis, persecution mania or something, but—well, yes, frankly, I think he is. Only not the same kind as Mr Spottiswoode. Uncle Harry's the rather nice, inefficient, sentimental sort of crook who always gets caught sooner or later."

"In which case we must hope that it's he who has stolen your father's diamond, and not Mr Spottiswoode," said Fen briskly. "I take it that theft is what you have in mind?"

"It's crazy, I know, and we shall probably find the diamond in the safe where Daddy put it. But—look, Professor Fen: Uncle Harry's meeting me at the house tomorrow morning to unlock the study and—and go through its contents. He's been in America up to five days ago, so there hasn't been a chance before. If I could just have someone with me. . . ."

And Fen nodded. "I'll come," he said. For he had known Ann Cargill long enough to be aware that, however erratic her views on *Beowulf* or Dryden, she was nobody's fool.

Uncle Harry proved to be a big, florid, amiable man dressed in checks with a black arm-band. And like his niece, he appeared at the Abingdon house next morning with a companion.

"Humbleby!" said Fen, pleased; and: "Well, well," said Detective Inspector Humbleby of Scotland Yard as he shook Fen's hand: "And what are you doing here?"

"Looking for a diamond," said Fen. "Miss Cargill is a pupil of mine . . . Ann, meet the inspector."

"We're all looking for a diamond," said Uncle Harry. "And from what the inspector told me yesterday, there's a damn good chance we shan't find one."

"Twenty thousand pounds," said Humbleby, "is somewhere about what the average high-class fence would give for a diamond like your father's, Miss Cargill. And £20,000 is what Mr Spottiswoode's executors found hidden in his house after his death. Being honest men, they came and had a word with us about it at the Yard. We've been working on the case for a fortnight now, and we still don't know where that money came from. Nothing legitimate, you can be sure . . .

"But there was never any secret about your father's buying that jewel; and his death was reported in the papers; and his name was on the list of Mr Spottiswoode's clients. So of course we started putting two and two together, and yesterday I had a word with your uncle about it, and he very kindly invited me down here, subject to your having no objection——"

"Of course not," said Ann.

"So that now," Humbleby concluded, "we shall see what we shall see."

A woman, Ann explained, had been coming in once or twice a week to keep the house dusted, but her ministrations had not, of course, included the study, which would undoubtedly be in a mess. And so it turned out.

When Uncle Harry had manipulated the elaborate locks, thrown the study door open and switched on the lights (for the room was in darkness, thanks to the solid steel shutters on the windows), they saw that dust—five weeks' dust—lay undisturbed on the furniture, the bare polished boards of the floor, everything.

Also it was cold in there: while Uncle Harry fumbled with the safe, Ann turned on the big electric fire and stood warming her hands at it. Presently, Fen, who had been peering at the marks left by their feet on the dusty floor, lifted his head and sniffed.

"Is there something burning?" he asked suspiciously.

They all sniffed. "I can't smell anything," said Ann. "Nor me," said Humbleby. "Nor me," said Uncle Harry, pausing in his labour: and added ruefully, "But then, it's years since I was able to smell anything."

Fen shrugged. "My mistake," he said. Though as a matter of fact it had not been a mistake, since he himself had not been able to smell anything burning, either. His eye caught Humbleby's. "Dog," he confided solemnly, "in the night-time."

Humbleby scowled. "Dog in the——"

"Eureka!" said Uncle Harry inaccurately: actually, all he had contrived to do so far was to get the safe door open. But a moment later he emerged from it holding a handsome jewel-box. "Would this be——"

"Yes, that's it," said Ann. "Open it, please."

And Uncle Harry opened it. And it was empty.

"It couldn't," Humbleby suggested, "be somewhere else?"

"No." Ann shook her head decisively. "I was with my father just before he left, and that was where he put it."

Uncle Harry grunted. "Anyway, there's your explanation of Spottiswoode's £20,000."

But Fen apparently did not agree. "No," he said. "Insufflator."

"Beg pardon?"

"Insufflator. For example, one of those rubber-bulb things barbers use for blowing powder on to your chin. And dust, as such, isn't really very hard to come by. It would take a little time, and a little care, but I'm willing to bet that given 24 hours you could re-dust the entire room."

An ugly gleam had appeared in Uncle Harry's eye. "Just what," he enunciated slowly, "are you suggesting?"

"I was suggesting a likely means for you to have used to cover up your traces after stealing the diamond. You stole it last night, I suppose, after Humbleby's account of Spottiswoode's hoard—which I should guess is probably blackmail money accumulated over a good many years—had suggested to you how you could disperse the blame. As to why Spottiswoode didn't forestall you—well, it may simply be that he didn't know of any means of disposing of such a distinctive stone."

"The man's mad," said Uncle Harry, with conviction. "Now look, sir: granted I *could* have stolen the diamond and then covered my traces with all this—this insufflator rubbish, what the devil makes you think I actually *did*? Where's your evidence, man, your proof?"

"The dog in the Sherlock Holmes story," said Fen, "did nothing in the night-time. And that was the curious incident."

"*Dog?*"

"Like this electric fire, here," Fen explained. "No smell of burning, you recall, when it was first switched on. But there *ought* to have been a smell of burning if the fire had been accumulating dust since (at the latest) Spottiswoode's death three weeks ago. Ask any housewife. Ergo, the fire had been very recently used. . . .

"And I'm afraid, Mr Cargill, that that means you."

MAN OVERBOARD

"BLACKMAILERS?" Detective Inspector Humbleby finished his coffee and began groping in his pocket for a cheroot.

"Well, yes, one does of course come across them from time to time. And although you may be surprised to hear this, in my experience they're generally rather nicer than any other kind of crook.

"Writers of fiction get very heated and indignant about blackmail. Yet, by and large, it's always seemed to me personally to be one of the least odious and most socially useful of crimes. To be a blackmailer's victim you do almost invariably have to be *guilty* of something or other. I mean that, unlike coshing and larceny and embezzlement and so forth, blackmail has a—a punitive function——

"Naturally, I'm not claiming that it ought to be encouraged." Having at last disinterred his cheroot, Humbleby proceeded to light it. "At the Yard, we have plenty of occasions for thinking that we're being deprived of evidence against a suspect in order that someone else may use it for private profit.

"On the other hand, a blackmailer can *acquire* such evidence more easily than we can—not having Judges' Rules to hamper him—and like Socrates in the syllogism, he's mortal. The death of a known blackmailer is a great event for us, I can tell you. It's astonishing the number of 'Unsolved' files that can be tidied up by a quick run through the deceased's papers. Sometimes even murders—Saul Colonna, for instance; we'd never have hanged him if a blackmailer hadn't ferreted out an incriminating letter and then got himself run over by a bus."

"Two Armagnacs, please," Gervase Fen said to the club waiter. "Colonna? The name's vaguely familiar, but I can't remember any details."

"It was interesting," said Humbleby, "because the incriminating letter didn't on the surface *look* incriminating at all . . . There were these two brothers, you see, Americans, Saul and Harry Colonna. They came over here—their first visit to

England—early in April of 1951, Saul to work in the office of the London correspondent of a Chicago paper, Harry to write a novel.

"New country—fresh beginning. But they'd hardly had a chance to unpack before Harry succumbed at long last to the cumulative effects of his daily bottle of Bourbon. With the result that *his* first few weeks among the Limeys were spent at a sanatorium in South Wales—Carmarthenshire, to be exact: no alcohol, no tobacco, lots of milk to drink, regular brisk walks in the surrounding countryside—you know the sort of thing.

"Harry didn't like that very much. His brisk walks tended to be in the direction of pubs. But at the same time he did acquire an awe, amounting almost to positive fear, of the formidable old doctor who ran the place. So that when at last he decided that he couldn't stand the régime any longer, he felt constrained to arrange for a rather more than ordinarily unobtrusive departure, such as wouldn't involve him in having to face a lot of reproaches for his failure to stay the course. Quite simply, abandoning his belongings, he went out for one of his walks and failed to return.

"That was on the afternoon of 7 May. About mid-day next day, *both* brothers arrived by car at Brixham in Devon, where they took rooms at the Bolton Hotel; for after only a month's journalism Saul had been sacked, and so had been free to respond to Harry's SOS from the sanatorium, and to assist in his flight. Once in Brixham, they proceeded to enjoy themselves. Among other things, they bought, actually *bought*, a small Bermudan sloop. And did quite a lot of sailing in it . . .

"Then, on the evening of the 12th, having ignored numerous warnings from the weather-wise, they got themselves swept out into mid-Channel by a gale. And in the turmoil of wind and darkness Harry was knocked overboard by the boom and drowned.

"That, at least, was Saul's account of the matter, when the Dartmouth lifeboat picked him up; and it was a credible story enough. Even the subsequent discovery that Harry's life had been well insured, and that Saul was the beneficiary, failed to shake it. If a crime *had* been committed, it was undetectable, the police found—with the inevitable result that in due course the insurance companies had to pay up. As to the body, what was left of that came up in a trawl about the beginning of September, near Start Point. By then there wasn't much chance of diagnosing the cause of death. But the teeth identified it as Harry Colonna beyond any reasonable doubt . . .

"So that without Laking, that would have been the end of that.

"Barney Laking was clever. He was a professional, of course. Though he'd been inside several times, he always went straight back to blackmail as soon as he'd done his term . . . So you can imagine that when a number 88 ran over him, in Whitehall, we lost no time at all getting to his house. And that was where, among a lot of other very interesting stuff, we found the let-ter—*the* letter.

"To start with, we couldn't make anything of it at all. Even after we'd linked the 'Harry' of the signature with Harry Colonna, it was still a long while before we could make out what Barney had wanted with the thing. However, we did see the light eventually . . . Wait and I'll do you a copy."

And Humbleby produced a notebook and began to write. "I looked at that letter so hard and so often," he murmured, "that it's engraved on my heart . . ."

"Envelope with it?" Fen asked.

"No, no envelope. Incidentally, for the record, our hand-writing people were unanimous that Harry Colonna *had* written it—that it wasn't a forgery, I mean—and also that nothing in it had subsequently been added or erased or altered . . . There."

And Humbleby tore the sheet out and handed it to Fen, who read:

You-Know-Where,
6.5.51

Dear Saul,
I'm just about fed with this dump: time I moved. When you get this, drop everything and bring the car to a little place five or six miles from here called Llanegwad (County Carmarthen). There's a beer-house called the Rose, where I risked a small drink this morning: from 6 on I'll be in it: Private Bar (so-called). Seriously, if I don't move around a bit I'll go nuts. This is URGENT.

Harry.

"M'm," said Fen. "Yes. I notice one thing."

"Actually, there are two things to notice."

"Are there? All right. But finish the story first."

"The rest's short if not sweet," said Humbleby. "We had Saul along and confronted him with the letter, and of course he said exactly what you'd expect—that this was the SOS Harry had sent him from the sanatorium, properly dated and with the distance from Llanegwad correct and so on and so forth. So then we arrested him."

"For murder?"

"Not to start with, no. Just for conspiracy to defraud the insurance companies."

"I see . . . Part of it is simple, of course," said Fen, who was still examining Humbleby's scrawl. "When an American uses '6.5.51', in writing to another American, he means not the 6th of May but the 5th of June . . . On the other hand, Saul and Harry, having settled in England, may have decided that it would save confusion if they used the English system of dating all the time."

"Which is just what Saul—when we pointed the problem out to him—told us they had decided to do." Humbleby shook his head sadly. "Not that it helped the poor chap."

Fen considered the letter again. And then suddenly he chuckled.

"Don't tell me," he said, "that 6 May 1951, was a *Sunday*?"

"Bull's eye. It was. Sunday in Wales. No pubs open for Harry to have even the smallest of small drinks at. Therefore, Harry was using the American system of dating, and his letter was written on 5 June, four weeks after he was supposed to have been swept overboard into the Channel. Insurance fraud."

"And Harry getting restive in his hideout near the sanatorium, and Saul suddenly thinking how nice it would be not to have to share the insurance money . . ."

"So back to Brixham, unobtrusively, by night, and out to sea again in the sloop. And that time," Humbleby concluded, "Harry really did go overboard."

"And you have found enough evidence for a murder charge?"

"As soon as we stopped worrying about 12 May, and started concentrating on the period after 5 June, we most certainly did. Mind you, it *could* have been difficult. But luckily Saul had had the cabin of the sloop revarnished at the end of May, and we found human blood on top of the new varnish—not much, after all that time, but enough to establish that it belonged to Harry's rather unusual group and sub-groups. Taken with the other things, that convinced the jury all right. And they hanged him . . .

"But you see now why I'm sometimes inclined to say a kind work for people like Barney Laking. Because really, you know, the credit in the Colonna case was all his.

"Even if I'd possessed that letter at the outset, I could quite easily have missed its significance. I only worked hard on it because it had come from Barney's collection, and I knew he didn't accumulate other people's correspondence just for fun.

"But *he* had no such inducement, bless him. With him it was just a consummate natural talent for smelling out even the most—the most deodorized of rats. What a detective the man would have made . . . Do you know, they gave me a full month's leave at the end of that case, as a reward for handling it so brilliantly? And it was all thanks to Barney . . ."

And Humbleby reached for his glass. "No, Gervase, I don't care what novelists say. I like blackmailers. Salt of the earth. Here's to them."

THE UNDRAPED TORSO

ERICSON—WHO WAS a photographer more or less permanently attached to that flourishing weekly magazine, *Pictures*—came into the cocktail bar of the Splendide at Dirlham-on-Sea that summer evening with a nasty welt visible just under his left eye.

"What happened?" Gervase Fen signalled the barman for another Martini. "Did you run into a door? Or is it just that some holiday-maker didn't want to be circulated to two million households in company with his neighbour's wife?"

"Actually, neither." Ericson took the glass from the barman and drank gratefully. "Thanks. Cheers . . . Your second guess gets near it, though. And look," he added defensively, "for heaven's sake don't go imagining that if it *had* been a matter of someone else's wife, I shouldn't have willingly given the chap the negative to destroy. I'm human. I don't go out of my way to make trouble for people . . ."

He brooded. "But this man was *alone*. That's one of the things that make it so odd."

"Did he smash your camera?"

"He did. And when they get angry enough or frightened enough to want to do that (this chap was more frightened than angry, I'm inclined to think), I just step aside and let them get on with it. They can almost always be made to pay . . . He paid, anyway. Took me back to his house and wrote a cheque. He was quite apologetic, too, after he'd cooled down a bit. Said he was sorry, but he just hated to have his picture taken."

"Some people do," said Fen. "There isn't necessarily anything suspicious about it."

"Agreed, agreed. But in his case there's more to it than just that: there are some things I haven't told you yet—enough to make me go along to the office of the local paper this afternoon and make some enquiries.

"He's a resident here, you see, not a visitor. Age about fifty. Name of Edgar Boynton. Unmarried. Settled here five years ago. Independent income—nothing spectacular, apparently, but more than enough for comfort. By way of being a prominent citizen, too—ex-councillor, sits on half a dozen committees, a patron of the hospital, all that sort of nonsense.

"And here's the queer thing: *he's never objected to being photographed before*—in fact, being on the smug side, he positively encouraged it. He actually had his picture in one of the national papers not so long ago, and they say he was as pleased as Punch."

Fen was interested. "Exactly what was this picture you took?" he enquired.

"Oh, the usual sort of thing you get on the beach. Only about eight people in it altogether. Kids making a sandcastle. Old lady in a deckchair. A couple of girls with a beach-ball. And in the foreground, Boynton lying on his back in the sand in bathing-trunks."

"M'm," said Fen. "Some people are a bit sensitive about their figures, you know."

"No need for him to be. For a man of his age he's in wonderful shape. And here's another odd thing: when I took that picture he had a newspaper spread over his face."

Fen stared. "That really does make it extraordinary. Unless—were there any distinguishing marks on his body?"

"Not one." Ericson assured him. "Not a mole or a tattoo or anything."

"Perhaps," Fen mused, "there *ought* to have been something—but in that case he'd hardly have dared to appear undressed in public at all . . . So what it boils down to is that here we have a man who doesn't mind having his face seen and photographed; and who doesn't mind having his body (on which there are absolutely no identifying marks) *seen*—but who's frightened enough to break an expensive camera when someone takes a picture of it."

He reflected. "I can think of one possible explanation of that. Tell me, is there anything unusual about Boynton's face?"

It was Ericson's turn to stare. "Yes," he said. "Though it beats me how you guessed it. Boynton's face has been pretty thoroughly patched up at some time in the past. Car-crash, he says. But what does that prove?"

"Nothing," said Fen pensively. "Nothing—yet. But I say,

Ericson, I'm getting very bored with Dirlham. I think I shall go off on my own for a few days."

Informed of this decision, Fen's family accepted it with resignation. Ever since their arrival they had observed the signs of restiveness mounting, and they knew that no protest was likely to do any good.

On the following morning, therefore, Fen took a train to London, where he contacted an old friend at Scotland Yard. Subsequently, having acquired there the information he sought, he paid a visit to an elderly widow, a Mrs Chandler, who lived alone in a cottage near Wycombe. Fen liked Mrs Chandler; it seemed to him a pity that the closing years of her life should have to be spent in an incessant struggle to make ends meet. So it was pleasant to be in a position to help her . . .

Back in Dirlham, he telephoned Ericson at the office of *Pictures*.

"Can you get down here for a night?" he enquired. "What I want . . ." And he proceeded to explain. From the other end of the wire came strangled cries.

"Look," said Ericson, when at last he was articulate again. "I have a job to hold down. Lord love us, Professor, if I try anything like that I'll have had it, for good. Look——"

"I'll come with you," said Fen reassuringly, "and if there's any trouble, I'll shoulder it. But there won't be any trouble for the simple reason . . ." and for a couple of minutes he talked almost without interruption.

"Well, that's different," said Ericson, finally. "I still don't like it much, but—all right, I'll come. Wait, though: doesn't he go down to the beach any more?"

"No. Not in bathing-trunks, anyway. That once was enough. He isn't risking any more prowling photographers."

"Okay, I'll buy it," said Ericson. "Hang on while I look up a train."

With the result that next evening, when Edgar Boynton went to his bathroom to take his regular six o'clock bath, a flash bulb suddenly illuminated him from behind the macintosh curtains of the shower, and simultaneously a shutter clicked. Mr Boynton was not pleased at this, and showed it. But thanks to a previously worked-out plan of campaign, the intruders contrived to escape from the house unharmed, and by eight, when a constable arrived to take them along to the police station, they were drinking innocently together in the bar of the Splendide.

At the police station they found not only an Outraged Citizen with a serious complaint to make, but also a neat, greying man with a cheroot in his mouth who was introduced to Ericson as Detective Inspector Humbleby of Scotland Yard.

"First and foremost," Boynton was saying, "I must insist that the film be handed over to me untouched. After that——"

"But it's already been developed, you know," Fen told him. "And printed."

Boynton paused, licking his lips. Then, speaking with markedly less assurance, he said: "Hand me that material—all of it—and I shall perhaps be prepared to overlook this disgraceful prank, and to proceed no further in the matter."

Fen, who had done the developing and printing himself, using Ericson's apparatus, produced an envelope. "Here it is. But I think that before I let you have it, Inspector Humbleby here may perhaps be interested to see——"

That was when Boynton turned and tried to run. But a constable, forewarned, put out a foot and tripped him—completing the manoeuvre, to everyone's great admiration, by contriving to catch his victim before he hit the floor.

"I'm afraid, sir, that we must ask you to remain here for further questioning," said the local inspector, not without relish. "Our information is that your real name is not Edgar Boynton, but James Bennett. And I must warn you——"

But Bennett alias Boynton heard nothing after that. He had fainted.

Later, over supper, Fen said: "He'd done time, you see, for stealing the Chandler jewels, back in 1934; but the jewels themselves were never recovered. . . . A pity he wanted to live a respectable life: ambition, to my mind, should be made of sterner stuff.

"However, since that was what he wanted, clearly a little plastic surgery had to be done on his face, in case anyone should recognize him and start enquiring into the original source of the income he was living on so comfortably.

"I'm afraid he's not going to be quite so well off from now on, because the law doesn't allow a man to profit from his crime, even after he's been punished for it, and so of course the value of the jewels, or as much of it as possible, will be recovered from him and given to Chandler's widow, who, as it happens, can do with it—which, of course, was just what he was afraid of. That was why he smashed your camera."

"Listen," said Ericson, "there just was no distinguishing mark on that man's body. None."

"To the naked eye, no. But now look at this picture you took of him in his bathroom."

"About time, too. . . ." Ericson gazed, then whistled. "Well, well. Quite a distinctive scar, that one; faint, but it's there all right. You mean——"

"I mean that black-and-white photography always emphasizes all reds and browns: the camera can see a healed-over scar where the eye can't. It really did seem the likeliest thing, you know— so what I did, of course, was to get hold of a sample of his fingerprints and take it to Scotland Yard. James Bennett, ten years for theft, loot never recovered. Unusual zig-zag wound across the ribs acquired while resisting arrest——

"Easy, isn't it? Once you know."

WOLF!

"THE ASS OF the philosopher Buridan," said Detective Inspector Humbleby, "on being placed precisely mid-way between two
equally succulent bundles of hay, was unable to see any logical
reason why it should proceed towards the one rather than the
other; and consequently starved to death. It's rather like that
with the Tidgwick case."

He frowned. "You're at liberty, of course, to say that the
comparison between myself and Buridan's futile creature isn't
very apt——"

"On the contrary——"

"—but the fact remains that as between robbery with violence
on the one hand, and a calculated parricide on the other, I can't
for the moment see anything to choose. Of course, as soon as we
go into the thing in detail, the scales are bound to come down on
one side or the other. But it would save a lot of time and trouble if
I could make up my mind which to concentrate on first. You
probably know in outline what happened. . . ."

"In very sketchy outline, yes," said his companion, whose
name was Gervase Fen. "I know that Tidgwick was a rich old
gentleman who got shot through the heart yesterday evening in
his own sitting-room. And I seem to remember the papers saying
something about his being well-known among his friends as a
practical joker."

" 'Notorious' would have been nearer the mark," said
Humbleby. "He really does seem to have been a quite remarkably silly old person. And the trouble is, it's this silliness of his
which has been responsible for confusing the issue. . . .

"Was he in fact murdered while he was talking to his elder son
on the telephone? Or was that just another of his jokes?

"Harold"—Humbleby went on—"Harold Tidgwick, this elder
son I've just mentioned, is a successful businessman with an
over-developed conscience. His brother Mortimer—a tubby,
cheerful young fellow with big winking glasses—is a research
physicist. Their father's estate, now that he's dead, will be

divided equally between them. But so far as I've been able to find out, it's only Mortimer who's in any immediate need of money. Mortimer, it appears, has an appetite for material luxuries somewhat in excess of his income, and that makes him my suspect number one."

"Your suspect number two, I gather, being some so far anonymous thug."

"Exactly. As to Harold, he's out of it, as you'll see in a moment. Now then, here's what happened.

"Yesterday evening, at precisely 10 pm, Harold Tidgwick received a telephone call from his father. For a minute or so they chatted about a dinner arrangement. Then Tidgwick *père* suddenly let out a yelp, and bawled something incoherent about someone 'coming at him', and then there was a second yell, and a shot, and a bump presumably caused by the telephone falling out of his hand.

"After that, nothing.

"Knowing the old man, anyone less conscientious than Harold would have dismissed this performance as bogus without a second thought. But Harold was too much the worrying sort to just let it pass, and after a little hesitation he rang Mortimer to ask him to go round to the father's house and make sure everything was all right."

"I should have thought," Fen interposed, "that Harold himself——"

"He had visitors in," Humbleby explained. "And it's they, by the way, who alibi him, for the whole evening. . . . Mortimer was sceptical, of course, when he heard what had happened, and argued the point. But in the end he gave in and went.

"What he found, on arriving at the house at about 10.15, you already know: the old man sprawled on the carpet, with the telephone receiver off its cradle beside him and the gun lying near his foot. . . . At least," Humbleby corrected himself, "that's what he says he found. And that, certainly, is what the DDI found twenty minutes later—Mortimer having phoned the police station from a box outside. But since Mortimer visited the house quite alone, there's no knowing. . . ."

"Exactly." Fen nodded. "By the way, how did he get in?"

"Through the back door, apparently. It was the manservant's night out, and the back door had been left open for when he returned. . . . No fingerprints. No other helpful traces. No difficulty about unobserved ingress or egress. . . .

"And that leaves just two possible hypotheses as to what happened.

"Number one: the telephone-call to Harold was genuine, and Tidgwick really was murdered at about a minute past ten. If that's so, it lets Mortimer out, because we've established definitely that he was at home at that time.

"Number two: the call to Harold was a practical joke, and Mortimer, taking advantage of the—um—putative alibi it would give him, murdered his father on arrival at 10.15."

"There's a third, isn't there?" said Fen. "Namely, that the call was bogus, but that none the less someone other than Mortimer shot Tidgwick before 10.15."

Humbleby shook his head, however.

"No. It won't wash. You see, old Tidgwick's house is semi-detached, with only a very thin dividing-wall between the Tidgwick sitting-room and the sitting-room next door.

"In that next-door sitting-room, during the whole of the evening, sat a very pleasant and obviously reliable couple who can swear that only one shot was fired, the one at about a minute past ten, and that——"

"But didn't they do anything about it?" Fen demanded, staring incredulously.

"They didn't. They knew old Tidgwick. They'd been had that way before."

"Ah, I see. Like the story of the child who cried 'Wolf!' Well, but look here, if this couple heard only the one shot, that lets Mortimer out."

"Wait, wait," said Humbleby. "Let me finish, please. The point is that just before 10.15—and they're certain of the time—this couple went out to have a nightcap at a pub. So if Mortimer did shoot his father, they would have just missed hearing it. . . .

"No: it's either some unknown, at a minute past ten. Or else it's Mortimer, at 10.15 or shortly after. And I'm damned if I know which."

There was a brief silence. Then Fen said abruptly:

"It has to be Mortimer, you know."

" 'Has to be'?"

"On the evidence you've given me, yes. Look at it this way. I think we can agree that an anonymous burglar——" Fen paused as a new thought occurred to him. "Incidentally, was there anything taken?"

"Yes. But Mortimer could have arranged that, as a blind. He had time enough, before the DDI arrived."

"Just so. Well then, I think we can agree that a burglar might well, after committing the murder, have replaced the fallen telephone-receiver in its cradle. But why, before leaving, should he change his mind and throw the thing back on the floor?"

"One can see why Mortimer, if guilty, would do that. If Tidgwick's call to Harold was a practical joke, then Tidgwick would have replaced his own receiver as soon as Harold rang off; and Mortimer would have thrown it on the floor again in order to give colour to the idea of the murder's having been committed at a minute past ten, a time for which he himself had an alibi."

Fen reflected. "He'd also, no doubt, get rid of the blank-cartridge pistol or whatever it was that Tidgwick used for his silly joke. That's a line, Humbleby. If you were to search about a bit——"

"Yes, yes," said Humbleby impatiently. "I can quite see that once we've proved the phone-call bogus, Mortimer hasn't got a chance. But what's all this about the telephone itself? I agree that if the receiver in old Tidgwick's room was replaced and then removed again, then obviously it's Mortimer who's guilty. But what on earth makes you think that happened? Why shouldn't the receiver have gone on lying on the floor continuously from 10.1 to 10.15? What proof is there that it didn't?"

And Fen sighed. "Our automatic telephone system," he said, "is a wonderful thing. Don't you see, Humbleby? If old Tidgwick's receiver was off from 10.1 to 10.15—if, in short, it was never returned to its cradle after Tidgwick picked it up in order to ring Harold, then Harold could never have phoned Mortimer or anyone else: you put people's telephones out of action if you don't ring off at the end of a call.

"But Harold did phone Mortimer. Therefore old Tidgwick's telephone was returned to its cradle after the bogus call. Therefore—again—it was subsequently put back on the floor for the police to find. And since no burglar could have any conceivable reason for doing that. . . .

"Simple, isn't it? Simple enough to hang a man."